THE LADY HAS A SCAR

THE CLASSIC HANK JANSON

The first original Hank Janson book appeared in 1946, and the last in 1971. However, the classic era on which we are focusing in the Telos reissue series lasted from 1946 to 1953. The following is a checklist of those books, which were subdivided into five main series and a number of 'specials'.

PRE-SERIES BOOKS
When Dames Get Tough (1946)
Scarred Faces (1947)

SERIES ONE
1) This Woman Is Death (1948)
2) Lady, Mind That Corpse (1948)
3) Gun Moll For Hire (1948)
4) No Regrets For Clara (194)
5) Smart Girls Don't Talk (1949)
6) Lilies For My Lovely (1949)
7) Blonde On The Spot (1949)
8) Honey, Take My Gun (1949)
9) Sweetheart, Here's Your Grave (1949)
10) Gunsmoke In Her Eyes (1949)
11) Angel, Shoot To Kill (1949)
12) Slay-Ride For Cutie (1949)

SERIES TWO
13) Sister, Don't Hate Me (1949)
14) Some Look Better Dead (1950)
15) Sweetie, Hold Me Tight (1950)
16) Torment For Trixie (1950)
17) Don't Dare Me, Sugar (1950)
18) The Lady Has A Scar (1950)
19) The Jane With The Green Eyes (1950)
20) Lola Brought Her Wreath (1950)
21) Lady, Toll The Bell (1950)
22) The Bride Wore Weeds (1950)
23) Don't Mourn Me Toots (1951)
24) This Dame Dies Soon (1951)

SERIES THREE
25) Baby, Don't Dare Squeal (1951)
26) Death Wore A Petticoat (1951)
27) Hotsy, You'll Be Chilled (1951)

28) It's Always Eve That Weeps (1951)
29) Frails Can Be So Tough (1951)
30) Milady Took The Rap (1951)
31) Women Hate Till Death (1951)
32) Broads Don't Scare Easy (1951)
33) Skirts Bring Me Sorrow (1951)
34) Sadie Don't Cry Now (1952)
35) The Filly Wore A Rod (1952)
36) Kill Her If You Can (1952)

SERIES FOUR
37) Murder (1952)
38) Conflict (1952)
39) Tension (1952)
40) Whiplash (1952)
41) Accused (1952)
42) Killer (1952)
43) Suspense (1952)
44) Pursuit (1953)
45) Vengeance (1953)
46) Torment (1953)
47) Amok (1953)
48) Corruption (1953)

SERIES 5
49) Silken Menace (1953)
50) Nyloned Avenger (1953)

SPECIALS
Auctioned (1952)
Persian Pride (1952)
Desert Fury (1953)
One Man In His Time (1953)
Unseen Assassin (1953)
Deadly Mission (1953)

THE LADY HAS A SCAR

HANK JANSON

This edition first published in the UK in 2013 by
Telos Publishing Ltd,
17 Pendre Avenue, Prestatyn, LL19 9SH,
www.telos.co.uk

Telos Publishing Ltd values feedback. Please e-mail us
with any comments you may have about this book to:
feedback@telos.co.uk

ISBN: 978-1-84583-873-7

Novel by Stephen D Frances
Cover by Reginald Heade
Silhouette device by Philip Mendoza
With thanks to Steve Holland

First published in England by S D Frances, 1950

British Library Cataloguing in Publication Data
A catalogue record of this book is available from the
British Library.

PUBLISHER'S NOTE

The appeal of the Hank Janson books to a modern readership lies not only in the quality of the storytelling, which is as powerfully compelling today as it was when they were first published, but also in the fascinating insight they afford into the attitudes, customs and morals of the 1940s and 1950s. We have therefore endeavoured to make *The Lady Has a Scar*, and all our other Hank Janson reissues, as faithful to the original editions as possible. Unlike some other publishers, who when reissuing vintage fiction have been known to edit it to remove aspects that might offend present-day sensibilities, we have left the original narrative absolutely intact.

The original editions of these classic Hank Janson titles made quite frequent use of phonetic 'Americanisms' such as 'kinda', 'gotta', 'wanna' and so on. Again, we have left these unchanged in the Telos Publishing Ltd reissues, to give readers as genuine as possible a taste of what it was like to read these books when they first came out, even though such devices have since become sorta out of fashion.

The only way in which we have amended the

original text has been to correct obvious lapses in spelling, grammar and punctuation, and to remedy clear typesetting errors.

Lastly, we should mention that we have made every effort to trace and acquire relevant copyrights in the various elements that make up this book. However, if anyone has any further information that they could provide in this regard, we would be very grateful to receive it.

The first reissue edition, in a maroon and silver cover with blue lettering.

The '7th Edition' version, in a dark and light blue cover with orange lettering.

1

I went to Hugh Burden's party only because Dane Morris suggested it.

There was no reason I should go except I was bored. My special friend, Sheila Lang, was in Florida judging a beauty contest and, of course, I'd never met Hugh Burden.

Unhurriedly I tooled the car along Milwaukee Avenue, past Binster's Golf Club and the Skyways Airport and out towards Burden's place.

Dane was silent, morose. He didn't look like a guy who was going to a party. He looked like he'd won a sweepstake but lost the ticket.

Dane was the *Chronicle*'s drama critic. He was a stocky, middle-aged guy with black hair smarmed back over his head. He wore a carefully-trimmed moustache, his cheeks were fleshy and his big, wide brown eyes were made beautiful by eyelashes that would have looked fine on a dame but somehow didn't go with the breadth of his shoulders. He wore a perpetual air of thoughtfulness, and when you talked with him he watched you with those big, wide eyes so thoughtfully you wondered if you were saying all the wrong things.

I wasn't altogether surprised Dane wasn't bubbling over with the joy of life. As the *Chronicle*'s drama critic he had to know a good deal about the theatre. He had to know a good deal about plays, the writing of plays and the people who acted in them. And much of his time he had to spend writing about Hugh Burden's plays.

That was where he felt the rub. Whatever else his faults were, there was no denying that Hugh Burden was a successful playwright. Right then, he was earning royalties from two plays playing simultaneously in Chicago and New York.

And they were good plays, too. The theatre world knew it, Hugh Burden knew it, the theatre financiers knew it and the box office returns showed the public knew it.

Dane Morris knew it, too. And since he was a newspaperman first and an individual afterwards, he wrote up those plays as they should be written up, acclaimed them and showered praise upon them.

But doing that made him sweat blood. You see, if there was anybody in the theatre world Dane had any reason to hate, for sure it was Hugh Burden.

Dane Morris had a regular job on the *Chronicle*. He earned his food and shelter, and if he went carefully he sometimes had a few bucks over to buy a few drinks or to splash on a dame. But there'd been a time when Dane Morris was ambitious. He'd been aiming high, like five million guys in Chicago are doing all the time.

Yeah, the spark of ambition had burned deeply inside Dane Morris. His knowledge of the theatre, his stage-craft, his writing ability, plus unlimited labour had at last resulted in one of his own countless plays being presented on the Chicago boards.

It's a major achievement getting a play staged. It

shows a guy's got a lot of ability, a lot of ingenuity, a lot of influence and a great deal of luck.

And when Dane's play finally achieved the distinction of being produced, the first of his ambitions had been realised.

But getting a play produced is only one half of the battle. The second half is making that play cover its expenses.

It's been said anybody can write a play, but it takes a genius to get it produced. Like all these clever sayings, it ain't exactly true. But the theatre is just a business, like producing battleships is a business. There are wheels within wheels.

All kinds of wheels revolve behind the scenes. And they all have to be taken into account. A perfectly good play, acclaimed by the critics, may be brought off before the end of the first week due to a whim of fate. A spell of good weather, a big fight, or even bad advertising, can affect attendance the first few nights and the play is a failure.

On the other hand, a mediocre play may score heavily for reasons that are not even apparent to the promoters, and may continue running for two or three years.

Yeah, the destiny of a play is always in the balance. But when the wheels behind the scenes are operating, when there is manoeuvring and determination that one particular play shall not succeed, it stands a poor chance.

The chances were that Dane Morris's play was a good play. The chances were it would have had a good run. He wouldn't exactly have made his fortune from it. But the first rung of the ladder to fortune would have been climbed. There'd have been other plays, more royalties and – who knows? – perhaps immortality.

Dane didn't realise at first what had happened. His play came off at the end of the first week, and for the next two weeks he went around like a doomed man. His world had collapsed. But after a time he began to get a clear picture of what had happened. Casual words were dropped here and there by the chattering, gossipy theatre folk. And after that, careful enquiries put him wise.

In a nutshell, not only Dane's play but the whole of his future had been deliberately sabotaged. And the guy behind it was Hugh Burden.

Hugh Burden had his reasons without a doubt. He was an established playwright. He was jealous of his position and wary of competition. He must have seen in Dane's play the possibilities of real competition. So he went to work with the critics. Coercion, subtle suggestions and even in rare cases open bribery got Dane's play a bad press. Actors and actresses, encouraged by the possibilities of parts in one of Hugh Burden's plays shortly to be produced, acted disinterestedly and woodenly, knowing that the continuation of Dane's play might lose them a part in Burden's play, which would be sure to have a long run.

The Angel who had sponsored Dane's work was anxious to be a successful promoter. Just the whisper that he might be allowed to sponsor Burden's next play was sufficient to get him wildly excited. He carved down expenses, he starved Dane's play of advertising publicity, he economised on the cast, insisting on ruthless cutting and elimination of incidental characters.

With the prospect of being a Burden sponsor, the Angel was only too anxious to seize his opportunity at the end of the week of withdrawing Dane's play and transferring his financial resources to what promised to be a more profitable venture.

As I said before, the theatre's a business like all other industries. And cut-throat competition can be expected there in the same way that it can be expected from manufacturers competing to sell vacuum cleaners.

But it was tough on Dane. It didn't only lose him the opportunity of a lifetime. It lost him his future and killed that spark of ambition that had been burning so brightly inside him. In the theatre profession, as is so often the case, he was acclaimed as a drama critic but described as hopeless at play-writing.

But Dane had to go on living. And the salt was rubbed into his wounds. He had to go on writing about the theatre, and quite a lot of the time he was writing about Hugh Burden's plays. And they were good. Nobody could deny that. And so Dane had to acclaim this man who had destroyed his work and his only chance of obtaining success.

I wasn't surprised Dane wasn't looking bucked at the prospect of spending an evening at one of Burden's parties. But there was no way that he could avoid it. Burden's private life was as important as his theatrical life to the newspapers. What Burton did was news. And Dane's job was to collect that news.

Five miles past the airport, Dane said: 'Take the next road on the left and it's about a mile along, up the hill. You can't miss it. A big, white-stone house on the left.'

'I bet you hate that guy,' I said softly.

His face was impassive. He said in an even voice: 'I got over hating him a long while ago. You just have to take life the way it is.'

'Maybe there's lots of guys who aren't so philosophical as you,' I said. 'Sometime, some place,

Hugh Burden is gonna get himself in real trouble.'

'That's happening all the time,' he said drily.

I'd never met Hugh Burden, but I'd heard a lot about him. He was successful. But the trouble was he knew it. He didn't wait to be told he was good. He told everybody first. He'd made plenty of money and he told the whole wide world. If his best friend had a car and a chauffeur, Hugh Burden would get himself two cars and two chauffeurs. If his next-door neighbour built himself a swimming pool, Hugh Burden built himself a lake. He was that kinda guy. He always wanted to go one better than anyone else. No matter what it cost.

He was that way with dames, too. If any actress considered beautiful and attractive was said to be a perfect match for some guy other than Hugh Burden, he'd set out to prove it wasn't true. The trouble was, he had the personality to do it. He'd break up any engagement on the impulse of the minute, exercising his charms upon the dame of the moment until she knew he was the one man in the world for her. Dames are soft about guys like that. Each one forgot there'd been a procession of dames before her. They were charmed and dallied with by Burden as long as it pleased him, and then dropped with a bang. It took them months and years to gather up the scattered pieces of their broken hearts.

Not that Burden was particular about his conquests. He'd as readily woo a shop-girl for a night as a society dame for a week. He was that kinda guy. All was grist that came to his mill. Or, to put it another way, all was female that came to his flat. And did his mill grind! The best and the worst that went into Hugh Burden's love factory could not be so distinguished when finally ejected. All was unsuitable for further use for a very long time.

I was driving very slowly. The houses in this district were class. There was plenty of space around and between them, and you didn't live in this neck of the woods unless you also had a private yacht on the lake, a bungalow in Florida and a bank balance that took two clerks to keep check of.

'What the hell's biting you, Dane?' I said. 'You're squatting there like a broody hen. So you don't like the guy. But it's been that way a long time. You don't have to die of grief on account of it.'

'I'm not thinking about Burden,' he said.

I looked at him from the corner of my eye. 'Got behind with your rent?'

He shook his head. 'No,' he said quickly. 'It's worse than that. It's Stella.'

I sighed, nodded my head understandingly. 'Woman trouble, huh?'

He scowled. 'Bad trouble, I'm afraid.'

Stella Moore was a girl Dane had met just a year before. I knew he was planning on marrying her just as soon as he could add a few more dollars to his weekly pay cheque. I'd met her with Dane a coupla times, had drinks with them. She was a cute kid. Redheaded and vivacious. Adaptable, too. Her speciality was singing heartbreaking torch songs in nightclubs.

She had the husky kinda voice and the right kinda figure to sing those songs with pathos in her voice and unshed tears shining in her eyes so the customers got all soft and sentimental inside. But she could act, too, and during the past few months had been getting prominent parts in farce.

'There's one good remedy,' I said wisely. 'Just give her a good spanking. Dames need that from time to time.'

He scowled oven more darkly. 'It's gone beyond that,' he said. 'We don't see each other no more.'

I was surprised. I'd always felt those two would make a match.

'Serious?' I asked. 'Or just a quarrel?'

'Serious,' he said.

'I'm sorry,' I said sympathetically. 'I thought you two ...'

'So did I,' he said.

'You don't have to feel so bad about it,' I said comfortingly. 'Just humble your pride a little, ring her up, go and see her, tell her you're sorry it all happened.'

'D'you think I'm a damned fool?' he snapped. 'Don't you think I'd do that if it would help?'

'What's the trouble then?'

I saw his hands clench tightly. His knuckles stood out whitely. 'She's got it bad,' he said. 'She's got Burden trouble.'

I managed to keep control of myself. I said quietly, 'You mean, she and Burden?'

'Started a fortnight ago,' he said. 'That guy's influence over women is just uncanny. From the time he dated her, she broke it off with me.' He snapped his fingers. 'Just like that. Won't answer my letters, won't answer the door to me, won't speak to me on the telephone. Just as though I'd never known her.'

'And she's going with him?'

'Everywhere,' he said bitterly. 'Everywhere.'

Well, it was none of my business. No guy owns a dame and no dame owns a guy. Everybody's an individual. You can't make a dame love a guy. She either does or she doesn't.

I saw Burden's stone-white house, swung round

off the main drag and around up the long gravel drive to the front door. There were about two dozen cars parked out in front. I coasted into line with the others, switched off the engine, and climbed out.

'We're here,' I said.

Dane scowled through the windscreen. He was still scowling as he climbed out of the car.

'You're supposed to look happy,' I said. 'Remember? This is a party. You're gonna enjoy yourself, fella.'

'There's only one thing I'd really enjoy,' he said, and just for a moment the look on his face frightened me.

'Don't tell me,' I said. 'I'll guess.'

'You've guessed right,' he said. 'I'd like to kill Burden. I'd like to settle him once and for all.'

2

A pretty, chicory-coloured maid opened the door. She was wearing a short, white, belted frock, white shoes and a maid's cap. She held one finger to her lip for silence and beckoned us in.

Somebody was playing the piano, somebody who really knew how to finger the ivories. It was one of those dreamy, mysterious compositions of Debussy.

'Come right on in,' she whispered hoarsely. She pointed to a door on the left.

Dane and I stood quietly in the doorway. It was a big room, about the size of a skating rink. The walls were almost entirely composed of modern steel-framed windows. There was a very thick carpet, very little furniture and about 80 folk distributed around the room.

Although the party was yet young, already the haze of cigarette and cigar smoke was hanging heavy in the air. Everybody had a drink in their hand and everywhere you looked there were decanters and plates of sandwiches.

But nobody was doing anything much except listening intently to the guy who was caressing the ivory keys of the big grand piano with long, sensitive fingers.

I nudged Dane. 'Look at that,' I whispered. I nodded my head.

'I know,' he said savagely. 'I know.'

Stella was leaning across the piano, her cheek resting on her hand and her glorious auburn hair glowing like a setting sun. There was a serene, happy look on her face and her eyes were staring dreamily into those of the piano-player. The way he looked at her you would have thought he was playing just for her alone and nobody else existed.

He wasn't the kinda guy you'd have liked to look at twice. He had thick black hair, cropped short so that it looked stubbly, and a rugged face with a square, hard jaw. He was wearing slacks and a crisp white shirt and his rolled-up sleeves showed strong, muscular arms covered with long, thick, curly hair. He was the last guy in the world you would have called a pretty boy.

But he sure could play. Most of the folks there were theatre folks. They weren't sensitive lilies. They weren't the type who would swoon in ecstasy at the sheer beauty of counterpoints. They were tough, hard-living, experienced folk, with brittle faces and hides like steel.

They weren't listening entranced for any other reason than that the music had really got them. And the reason it had got them was that the pianist was something special in the way of pianists.

I looked around. I nudged Dane again. 'Where's Burden?' I asked.

He nodded towards Stella. 'There,' he said.

'Burden,' I whispered. 'Not Stella.'

'That's him,' he said. 'Right there.'

I didn't believe it at first. That tough-looking guy couldn't be Burden the lady-killer. But when I looked a second time it began to grow upon me. Sure, he was tough. He was as ugly as an ape. But there's a savage strength about ugliness that appeals to some women. And there was something about Burden's eyes, too. There was something about his eyes when he looked up into Stella's face that counted. If you were a dame and looked into eyes like that you could forget his ugliness, sense only his rugged, primitive savageness. And ever since there were caves, dames have fallen for cavemen.

His appearance, too, fitted in with what I had heard about him. He was reckoned to be a tough guy. It was said that when Hugh Burden arrived in a nightclub, the manager rang up his insurance company, doubled his premium and sent for the doctor.

Burden was said to be the toughest guy south of Lake Michigan. He'd had more fights in nightclubs, listed more charges for assault than any other guy in theatre business. He had a pile of chips on his shoulder as high as the Woolworth building, and a gentle draught of criticism would send them tumbling.

He had a volcanic temper. He'd launch into action, batter and bash with his bare hands until his rage subsided.

And I was watching the guy right now. He was a successful playwright. He charmed women so they swooned at his feet, then he'd walk on them. He'd fight anybody on the strength of a causal remark. And right now he was playing Debussy with such exquisite tenderness and sensitivity everyone was listening with baited breath. Sure, he was some guy, this Burden. Some guy!

But not the type I like!

'So that's the guy,' I breathed.

'That's him,' said Dane bitterly.

'Could do with having his face lifted,' I said.

'Use a crack like that and he'll push your teeth down your throat,' warned Dane.

'If I didn't bite his hand off at the wrist first,' I retorted.

The lingering, soulful notes twined into a cascade of uniting treble and bass. The final chords rung out, throbbed on the air, softly sighed into silence.

There was a kinda satisfied sigh of relaxation and then everybody applauded. Burden was still looking into Stella's eyes, his fingers still resting on the keys. She lifted her glass, sipped it, and then held it to his lips. When he drank he still didn't take his eyes from hers.

Dane drew a deep, angry breath.

There was talking now, animated conversation and the clink of glasses. Sandwiches and fruit were being passed around.

Maybe Burden felt Dane's eyes probing him. He looked up towards the doorway. He caught sight of Dane, and a sneer of malicious contempt was in his black eyes when he called out loudly: 'Hiya, Dane! Come right over.'

It was a tough spot for Dane. He was there for the *Chronicle*. He had to take it or quit his job. He was man enough to take it, and I admired him for it.

He took me by the arm and steered me across to the piano. He looked at Burden steadily, and said: 'Nice party, Hugh.'

'That's right,' said Burden. 'Nice party.' There was a kinda mocking twist to his lips. His eyes slipped sideways to me. 'I don't think –' he began.

'Hank Janson,' said Dane, 'You've heard of him. I guessed you wouldn't object –'

'Sure not,' said Burden heartily. He reached out a

hand, gripped mine. It was a hand that was strong, like steel. And in his eyes there was that same mocking contempt that he had for everyone. 'We must have a talk sometime,' he said. 'May I could use some of your news-paper experience to give a factual background to one of my plays.'

'It could be mutual,' I drawled. 'Maybe I could use some of your factual experience as a background for some of my news.'

The chip on his shoulder was as high as a barn. His eyes hardened. There were a dozen ways he could have taken my reply. Six of them could have been unpleasant.

This was Dane's party. It wouldn't be fair to start trouble right away. I grinned easily as though I intended the reply as a compliment. Burden's eyes lingered upon me for a moment and then the chip shrank to reasonable proportions. He half-turned around towards Stella and jerked his head. 'You know Stella?' he asked.

'Sure,' I said. 'I know Stella.' I nodded at her curtly. 'Having a good time?'

'Marvellous,' she drawled. She didn't take her eyes off Burden once.

Burden's black eyes were full of malicious contempt as he said to Dane, 'Meet Stella, Dane –' Then he broke off quickly. 'Oh, yeah. I forgot. You two used to know each other.'

'That's right,' said Dane. He spoke through his teeth, and his cheeks were flushed. He looked at Stella. 'How are you, Stella?'

'Fine,' she said abstractedly. 'Just fine.' She still kept looking at Burden like he was all the world to her.

'Well, what say you boys get some drinks?' said Burden. He looked around, called to one of the coloured maids. 'Hey, Brown Sugar. Over here.'

She brought over a tray of glasses filled with green-coloured liquid. We each took one – Stella, Burden, Dane and me.

'You'll like these,' said Burden. 'A special. I invented it myself. Call it the Atomic Bomb.'

I sipped mine. It was good. It had enough sizzle in it to drive a rocket-plane half-way to the moon.

The coloured maid was still waiting. Burden waved his hand at her airily. 'Help yourself, Brownie.'

Her eyes widened.

'Go on,' he encouraged. 'Have a drink. This is a party, everybody's eating and drinking.'

She still didn't believe he was serious. She shook her head, smiling.

'What's this?' grinned Burden. 'Insubordination?' He took the tray from her hands, put it on the piano. He poured the green-coloured liquid from one glass into another so that the glass was filled to the brim. He turned to the maid, holding the glass carefully.

'There,' he said indulgently. 'Take a slug at this. It'll make you feel better.'

She didn't want it. But she hadn't the courage to refuse. She sipped it, shuddered, pulled a wry face and held the glass away from her as though afraid it would explode.

'Go on,' urged Burden. 'Drink it.'

I couldn't put my finger on it, but somehow there was a dominating tone in his voice. And the maid noticed it. She looked at him, steeled herself and then drank. And he stood over her, watching her, making sure she drank it to the last drop. By that time her eyes were filled with tears and she was wanting to hang out her tongue. She excused herself quickly, took the tray and bustled out of the room.

'I don't go for this colour bar,' said Burden loudly. 'I figure all guys are equal. Why shouldn't she enjoy the party like the rest of us?'

It was a laugh hearing that crack about all guys being equal. If ever a guy figured he was better than anyone else, it was Hugh Burden. You could tell that even while he was speaking. And just how he figured he was making the coloured girl enjoy herself by scorching her insides with liquor she didn't want, I just couldn't figure.

'A real Democrat,' I murmured.

'What's that?' he growled.

'You're a darling,' said Stella at the same time. For the last few moments he hadn't been looking at her. She couldn't bear that. She wanted to regain his interest. She came around, slipped her arm in his and stroked the thick black hairs on the back of his wrist.

'You played wonderfully, darling,' she said.

'Not bad at all, eh?' said Burden with satisfaction.

I caught Dane's eye. He jerked his head imperceptibly and drifted off. I trailed along after him. We left Burden and Stella staring into each other's eyes, saying sweet nothings.

'Another ten seconds and I'd have socked him,' said Dane.

'Listen to the philosopher,' I jeered. 'What the hell are you worried about, anyway? You're sore, sure. He's taken your dame. But if she's that easy for some other guy, what are you a-worrying about?'

He stood stock still, looked at me thoughtfully and moistened his lips. 'I'd just as soon sock you,' he said.

'Okay,' I said. 'Go ahead and sock me. That'll keep it in the family. We won't have the drama critic fired from the *Chronicle* for socking the famous playwright.'

His eyes softened. He patted my shoulder. 'Sorry, Hank,' he said. 'I guess I'm all mixed up.'

'Forget it,' I said.

There was a helluva lot of drinking going on. Spirits were flowing like water. Over in one corner, a fella was proving he could stand on his head. A gust of laughter came from another group of people, one of whom was giving a very good imitation of Neville Chamberlain. Somebody had switched on the radio and lots of folk were dancing.

A soulful-looking dame with closely cropped curly hair brushed against Dane as she tried to pass him with a glass in her hand.

'Sorry,' she said. She stopped. 'Oh, it's you, Dane,' she said. 'How nice to see you again.'

'You're looking swell,' he said. 'How are things going?'

The soulful eyes reflected worry. 'Just about the same, Dane.' She forced a smile.

Dane introduced me briefly. She was Dorothy Burden. She was the wife of Hugh Burden. That alone got me on her side immediately. Any dame married to that guy needed all the sympathy she could get.

'Is Charlie here?' asked Dane.

'Come over and meet him,' she said.

As we trailed along behind her, Dane whispered: 'Charlie Skinner's the guy she wants to marry.'

'Ain't one husband enough?'

'She quit Burden three years ago,' he said. 'Two months of married life was enough. More than enough, I guess.'

'Who's Charlie Skinner?'

'Nobody of importance,' he said. 'Real estate agent. Very little dough.'

'That why they can't get married?'

'Burden's the reason they can't get married,' he said. 'Won't let her divorce him. So there she is, dependent financially upon Burden, has to accept what little dough he gives her, and all the time she's eating her heart out for Skinner.'

Skinner was sitting away in the corner by himself. He looked out of place and lonely. His eyes lighted up when he saw Dorothy and turned to dull suspicion when he saw we were with her.

'You know Dane, don't you?' she said.

He nodded dourly. Then his eyes flicked to me.

'Mr Janson is a friend of Dane's,' she said. 'Just dropped in to get a bit of atmosphere, I guess.'

I shook hands with Charles. He was a tall, loose-limbed fella with a hank of black hair hanging carelessly across his forehead. He had a peculiar trick of talking with his mouth held wide open, hardly seeming to move his lips. He somehow gave the impression of being a schoolboy who'd grown up too rapidly, outgrown his strength and hadn't acquired confidence in himself.

'How's business?' I asked. Just something to say.

'Bad,' he said. His eyes wandered to Dorothy. It was as though he was frightened to say anything without first of all getting her unspoken consent.

'Things always get bad about this time,' I said conversationally. I felt I had to put this guy at his ease.

'You know how it is,' he said. 'Folks decide to buy. Let you draw up a whole lot of papers and then they back out. All your time wasted.'

His eyes looked at Dorothy again, and she smiled softly. He smiled sheepishly. It was as though she had said, *'Don't worry, Charles. I love you. You don't have to worry about anything.'*

The strains of a waltz were filling the room, and conversation was balancing on a pin-point. I figured Charles was shy and wanted softening up. Dane could do that. I turned to Dorothy and said, 'What say we kick this around?'

She slipped into my arms easily and she danced exceedingly well. After a coupla turns, she said: 'You're a friend of Dane's?'

'I've known him quite a time.'

She asked thoughtfully: 'Do you think he'll ever get a chance again?'

'Another play?'

She nodded.

'Not a chance,' I said. 'Throughout life everybody gets so many chances. If you miss out on them, you've lost them for good.'

'Such a pity,' she said. 'Dane's such a nice fella. If only Hugh –' She broke off as though she'd been about to say something she shouldn't have said.

'If only your husband wasn't so selfish, Dane would have had his chance,' I finished for her.

She was silent for a moment, and then said: 'You know about it, then?'

'Yeah,' I said bitterly. 'You sure picked yourself a fine husband.'

I was surprised at the venom in her voice. She just couldn't hold herself back. 'He's a swine,' she said. 'He's an absolute selfish swine!'

'I've heard about it,' I said gently. 'He won't give you a divorce.'

'He likes to torture me.'

'I can see the way it is between you and Charles,' I said sympathetically.

'He knows it, too,' she said bitterly. 'That's the only

reason he won't divorce me. Because he wants to see me suffer.'

'How did you get here, anyway?' I asked. 'Did he invite you?'

'Invite me! It was practically a command.'

It sounded an interesting situation. But if she was gonna talk it would be because she wanted and not because I pressed her. I just said: 'Yeah?' And waited.

'Money,' she said briefly. 'He's playing with us like a cat with a mouse. He worked through an agent, bought up the debentures on Charlie's business. He can ruin Charlie at any time. And that's just the way he likes it. He's got the whip-hand. He won't smash us, and he won't let us get away. He just dangles us on a string, leaving us in perpetual doubt.'

'And you have to do what he says, or else?'

'I have to be nice to him,' she said. 'I have to attend his parties. He drives me as near breaking point as he dares.'

'You missed your chance, lady,' I said. 'You should have stayed married to that guy. Put cyanide in his coffee.'

'Maybe sometime I'll even do that,' she said. And once again I was shocked by the intensity of hatred in her voice. For one moment I almost believed that she would do it.

'Charlie's a nice guy,' I said. I tried to be cheerful, change from the sullen tone.

'Yes.' She sighed and seemed to soften all over. 'Charlie's a real nice guy. If only …' She broke off.

'Yeah,' I said. 'If only he'd divorce you.'

'Or if someone would kill him,' she added, with sharp, sudden anger.

I laughed that off too. 'Sounds like you're gonna

give me a story for my paper.'

She laughed then. 'Stick around, Hank,' she said. 'Maybe you'll get that story.'

We drifted back to the corner where Charlie and Dane were discussing the previous week's ballgame with animated agitation. But as soon as Charles saw Dorothy his eyes lighted up and he kinda edged himself between me and her as though afraid I might take her away.

The party was getting really steamed up now. There was a fat guy near me, as broad as he was tall and about six deep in chins. His flabby cheeks were sweating and he was chuckling deep down in his belly as he unzipped the back of a girl's dress. The zip was a long one, reaching almost to the base of her spine, and she was wearing nothing beneath the dress. She was annoyed with the fat guy. She didn't mind the dress being unzipped, but he kept picking grapes from a fruit-dish and crushing them beneath his podgy thumb against her back so that the juice made her skin glisten.

She was kneeling down with a group of other people throwing dice. The fat guy's attentions so annoyed her that finally she appealed for help. Two or three of her friends worked on the fat guy, spread him on the floor and with a penknife cut off every button of his clothing. They made a thorough job of it. For the rest of the evening, the fat guy was wandering around with a doleful look on his fat face, clutching his trousers tightly to his paunch and trying to persuade somebody to find him a needle and cotton.

Burden was showing how democratic he was. He was dancing with one of the coloured maids. The same maid he had forced to drink his cocktail.

I don't know whether it was Burden's democratic

attitude or the cocktail that reduced to zero the gulf in society, but she didn't act like a maid anymore. She was dancing with a kinda dreamy look in her eyes, resting her head on his chest and with one hand gently caressing the back of his neck. Somewhere, she'd lost the maid's cap.

Stella was sitting by the piano, watching Burden with broody eyes. I saw Dane work around behind her and whisper something in her ear. He might not have been there for all the notice she took. He kept talking, and after a while he asked her a question. He asked the question about three times before she replied. She gave a kinda bored sigh and said just one word. I didn't have to be a lip-reader to know what it was. She'd said 'No' as emphatically and definitely as it's possible to use the word.

He did some more talking and then quite naturally put his hand on her shoulder. She flinched away from him, pushed his hand off her shoulder and flung it away from her as though it burned.

That did it. Dane drew himself up, his lips compressed, and he stalked away from her. I guess he wanted her to sense his contemptuous anger as he left her. But she didn't. She was watching Burden with soft, yearning eyes, and with just a hint of concern in them. She needed to be concerned, the way that coloured girl was pressing up against him.

Charles and Dorothy were dancing now. A tall, slim man with a weak chin and misty blue eyes blundered into me. 'I say, old fella,' he said in a thick voice that just managed to control his pronunciation. 'Have you tried this drink?'

He thrust a cocktail in my hand. The liquid was a sparkling golden yellow.

'What is it?' I asked.

'S'wonderful,' he told me. He had a glass himself. He drank half of it, swayed very, very lightly and closed one eye before he nodded his head approvingly.

'S'wonderful,' he repeated. 'Just try it.'

I tasted it. It had all the Atomic Bomb contained and more. I rolled it around my tongue, let it trickle down into my belly. It dripped on top of the Atomic Bomb, and pleasurable warmth and exhilaration mingled inside me.

'That really is something!' I said, approvingly. 'What is it?'

'Just invented it,' he said proudly. He raised his arm indicating the cocktail bar. 'Fella said, "Mix a cocktail", so I mixed it.' He held up the glassful of yellow liquid as though it was a great prize. 'Invented it – just like that!' he added.

'What are you going to call it?' I chuckled.

He considered the question, 'You like the other drink?'

'The Atomic Bomb?'

He nodded. 'The green drink. You like it?'

'Pretty good,' I said.

'This one is better?'

'Definitely,' I assured him.

'That's it,' he said. 'The other one is Atomic Bomb. I call mine World's End.'

'How d'ya make it?' I asked.

'It's very simple,' he said. He finished his drink, pulled back his cuff and prepared to tick off the items on his fingers. 'First you take some gin. Then you take some …' He broke off, and a thoughtful look came on his face. He started again. 'First you take some gin. Then you take some …' He broke off again.

'Vermouth?' I suggested gently.

'Maybe,' he said broodingly. 'It's a funny thing, that. It's the first time in my life I've ever invented anything. First time I've done anything worthwhile, and what happens? I've forgotten how I made it.'

I nudged him in the ribs consolingly. 'Well, there's two fellas who will remember it all their lives, isn't there?'

He grinned. 'You're a nice guy,' he said. 'I like you.'

'I'd take you up on it if you wore skirts,' I said.

'Let me introduce myself,' he said. He swayed again. This time quite obviously. He tested the air as though to lever himself into an upright position. 'My name's Fuller,' he said. 'Leslie Fuller.'

The name seemed familiar to me. 'Have I seen you around?'

'Sure to have done, old chap,' he assured me. He slapped his hand on my shoulder. 'I'm a washout, you know.' He stared at me solemnly. 'Loads of dough and all that. My father's dough, of course. He makes it. I spend it.'

The name was hitting me now. A Texas mine-owner, millionaire. A playboy son called Leslie. A good-for-nothing who'd never done an honest day's work, who ran up gambling bills that could have dried up his father's oil wells if he hadn't had more than a dozen.

'Gordon Fuller's son?' I asked.

'That's right,' he said. He slapped himself on the chest. 'I'm a washout,' he announced. 'No good to anybody. Waste money gambling. Spendthrift. You know the kinda fella I am. I'm no good to anyone.'

He was just the kinda guy who would be at one of Burden's parties. But I liked him better than Burden. At any rate, Leslie Fuller did know his own drawbacks.

'You ought to reform, fella,' I grinned. 'Ever tried growing oranges in Florida?'

He raised one finger to me. 'I'm going to reform. Got the sweetest little girl. She's going to reform me. I'm going to work hard. Be a different fella.'

He suddenly caught sight of somebody among the dancers. He dived into the scrum, grabbed the girl by the arm and pulled her out. She'd been dancing with Dane. She came out, laughing and protesting. Leslie said: 'Want you to meet the sweetest little girl. Going to make a man of me.'

'Leslie, you mustn't keep talking like that,' she reproached him. She had fair hair, a pretty blush to her cheeks and sparkling eyes. She added: 'Besides, you were so rude to my partner.'

Leslie was immediately contrite. 'My dear old fella,' he said to Dane. 'You understand, don't you? I just had to –'

'That's okay,' grinned Dane, 'You go ahead.'

'That's fine,' said Leslie. 'That's fine.' He looked at the girl thoughtfully, looked at Dane, and then looked at me. 'Now what was it?' he asked himself thoughtfully, and then his face cleared. 'Ah!' he said. 'You take a good measure of gin and then you take a …' His voice broke off, and he shook his head sadly.

'You were going to introduce us,' I reminded him gently.

His face lighted up again. 'Ah, yes, that's right. The prettiest, sweetest little girl –'

'Please, Leslie,' she dimpled.

He took her by the arm and turned her to face me. 'I want you to meet a good friend of mine, darling,' he said. 'I want you to meet …' His voice broke off again, and he looked at me anxiously.

'Janson is the name,' I said. 'Hank Janson.'

'Pearl,' she said. 'Pearl Gibbons,' and her cool fingers slipped into mine. I liked her eyes. They were cool, self-assured. In fact, her whole manner was cool and confident. You got the feeling she was just the kinda girl who could straighten out Leslie – if anyone could.

'Have you met Dane?' I asked.

She smiled at him. 'Not officially,' she admitted.

'Dane Morris,' I said. 'Drama critic on the *Chronicle*.'

Dane acknowledged her half-heartedly. Every now and again he glanced to the far end of the room, where Burden and Stella were sitting and looking into each other's eyes. Pearl's eyes rested on Dane thoughtfully.

Leslie said, 'Don't you mind me. You carry on dancing. I've got other things to do. I've got to mix a cocktail.'

Pearl looked at Dane. 'Would you like to?' she asked shyly.

He smiled back half-heartedly. She slipped into his arms and they drifted away into the maze of other dancers.

Leslie frowned. 'Gotta mix another cocktail,' he said. He said it as though it was a serious duty.

'You slip along then, fella,' I said. 'The bar's right over there.'

I turned him around, pointed him at the bar like he was a rifle and gave him a gentle push. He steered an erratic course across the room. But he made it. I watched him fumbling among the bottles with that perplexed look on his face. Deep down in his mind he was probably resolved to achieve the distinction of producing two inventions in one evening. I wondered what he'd call the next. Maybe it'd be called the Beginning.

A soft hand tugged at my arm, so that I turned around and looked down into a pair of fathomless black eyes.

'Hello,' she said, in a kinda little-girl voice.

'What's cooking?' I asked.

'I am,' she said. 'Just about ready to be served. Wanna take a bite?'

I looked her over. She was dark, just the right height, had the kinda figure that makes an unmarried man lie awake at night, and moist, warm, inviting lips that could sear at a touch.

'With you,' I said, 'I'm liable to forget my party manners and start in wolfing.'

She chuckled, gave a soft imitation of a wolf's howl and moved in close.

'Shall we dance first?' she asked.

'Only if it's absolutely necessary,' I grinned.

We drifted out among the other dancers. It was a slow foxtrot. The lights were on now – soft, soothing lights. I'd had three of those Atomic Bombs followed by a World's End, which had detonated on top of the others. A new atmosphere was coming into the party. An atmosphere of warm, cosy dreaminess. Her cheek was resting on my shoulder and her hair tickled my nose. From shoulder to thigh her body moulded into mine, following faithfully every movement I made. There was a tantalising scent in my nostrils and I could feel the sensuous movement of her body beneath her dress.

Suddenly it seemed a very nice party. I was beginning to enjoy myself after all, despite the little pinpricks.

'D'you know something, honey?' she asked.

'What?'

'Can you get a bit closer?'

'Not right here in front of everybody.'

'I wish you could,' she said regretfully. Then, after a few moments, she added: 'My, what a pressure-cooker you've turned out to be!'

3

She clutched me and I clutched her throughout the next three dances. Then we got separated.

I wandered across to the cocktail bar to fix myself another drink. I found Leslie Fuller, the playboy, seated against the wall behind the counter with his knees under his chin, fast asleep. He was nursing the cocktail-shaker to his breast like it was a baby.

I stepped over him, dived down behind the bar and came up with a bottle labelled Bourbon. That was good enough for me without mixing. I poured myself a generous five fingers, added a piece of ice and a split-second spurt from the siphon and found myself a chair.

The party was getting progressively hotter. Those kinda parties did. As the mineral spirits went down, so the animal spirits went up. Pearl, the sweet girl who was gonna save playboy Leslie Fuller from making a wreck of his life, was still dancing with Dane. She was looking up into his face like she'd never seen him before and couldn't get over her good luck at having found him at last. He was talking right back at her, smiling, and for the first time that evening looking happy. But, just the same, he still kept slipping swift glances across the room towards Hugh Burden and Stella, and when he did so he scowled momentarily.

You'd have thought Burden and Stella were alone, the way they acted. They were sitting on a settee. Her skirt was rucked up over her thighs, which were crossed, imprisoning Hugh's hand. Judging from the way he was nuzzling her neck, it didn't look like he wanted to get away, anyhow!

The coloured maid looked like she might have had two or three more Atomic Bombs. The dancers were jiving now and she was kicking twice as high as anybody. Her hair had got loosened and streamed over her shoulders as she bobbed up and down. She was sure working hard at it. Her face gleamed with perspiration, her eyes rolled and her white teeth flashed in a broad grin. There were sweat patches beneath her armpits and another sweat patch where the belt of her crisp, white linen frock was drawn tight around her belly.

There was a quiet little man seated next to me. I said conversationally, 'Looks like she's warming up.'

He looked at her gloomily. 'Yeah,' he said quietly. 'That's right.'

There was something pathetic about the guy. He was short on hair, and what he had was grey. He was maybe 50 or 60. His cheeks were sunken, his shoulders drooped, and when he turned his eyes to me I saw they were haggard.

'Something bothering you, chum?' I asked sympathetically.

He started like I'd pointed a gun at him. 'No,' he said quickly. 'I'm all right. There's nothing the matter, really.'

I didn't want to probe into private affairs, but he looked such a pathetic little guy I felt sorry for him. I wanted to cheer him up.

'Haven't I seen you before somewhere?' I asked.

'Maybe,' he said absently. 'I'm Mr Burden's personal secretary.'

I nodded understandingly. 'You have to sit through too many of these to get a kick out of it.'

'Unfortunately so,' he agreed. 'Only today I particularly wanted –' He broke off and looked around anxiously.

One of the coloured maids who was still working passed by collecting empty glasses. She had a couple of drinks on the tray. She offered one to the pathetic little guy.

He shook his head. Smiled his thanks.

'Have one,' I said. 'It'll cheer you up.'

'Never touch it,' he said. 'Doctor's orders.'

I showed the girl the three fingers of Bourbon I still had left. She flashed a smile and carried her tray to the next easy chair, which four dames were trying to sit in together with a loud-voiced guy wearing a loud-check suit.

The little guy next to me kept fluttering his hands nervously. He kept looking at Burden and he kept shooting quick glances at the clock.

'Why don't you scram?' I asked.

'I'll have to,' he confessed. 'But Mr Burden will be very annoyed with me if he finds out.'

'Tell him to go take a jump in the lake.'

He looked at me reproachfully. 'You must remember, I am only an employee.'

'Yeah,' I said quietly. 'I'd forgotten that.' And then I got an idea. 'Look,' I said. 'You wanna get away. You go. If he misses you, tell him I asked you to do something for me. My name's Janson.'

'What could I do for you?' he asked seriously.

I thought for a moment. 'Look,' I said. 'I work on the *Chronicle*. Tell him I wrote some copy for you. You had to take it along to the office for me. Say they kept you there if necessary.'

'That would help,' he said. He repeated my name thoughtfully. 'Are you quite sure it will be all right?'

'You've an excuse, anyway,' I said. 'And he might not miss you.'

'I'll have to go, anyway,' he said. He looked at the clock anxiously. 'They said I'd have to come back. They can't decide anything yet.' His haggard eyes looked at me. He was a guy who had a lot on his mind, and it wasn't just worry. There was something deeper than that.

'You slip off, chum,' I said. 'I'll cover up for you if you're wanted.'

He muttered more thanks and shuffled out. He was such a nondescript little guy that nobody noticed him going and nobody would have noticed him if he'd come in.

The jive session finished. They'd been going hard at it for nearly half an hour. Some of the guys took off their jackets and the dames stood around, fanning themselves with paper serviettes and surreptitiously wiping the perspiration from their faces.

That gave somebody a bright idea. Just the kinda bright idea the party was warmed up to appreciate. It was a game. It was striptease, and everybody loved the idea. Everybody stood around in a circle to play it, and everybody had to play it. It was that kinda game. If anybody was left out, it lost its point.

It was played like this. Everybody took turns at throwing the dice. There were two dice. And the number they threw was against them instead of for them.

Every article of clothing had a value. A man's jacket was four points, his waistcoat was three points, but his trousers were six points. A pair of underpants was worth nine points. There was a scale worked out for the dames, too. Luck decided if you lost your clothes, and then a forfeit would be imposed before you could get them back.

Burden sent one of the maids for a laundry basket, which was placed in the middle of the circle. Then the first guy in the circle took the dice-cup, shook the ivories and rolled a three and a four. That was seven points. He grinned, took off his coat, which was four points, and dropped it in the laundry basket. Then, glumly, he calculated how many more points he needed and with a rueful grin took off two shoes and one sock to make up the seven points.

That got quite a laugh. The guy grinned sheepishly and tried to make out he thought it funny, too. But when the next in line began to shake the ivories – she was a dame – his interest perked up. His laugh was louder than the others when she rolled two fours and pouted her dismay.

There was lots of shouted advice as to what she should do. She gave the matter consideration, kicked off her shoes, which earned her two points, and, with a shy giggle, wriggled out of her blouse. She was wearing an underslip and brassiere, but just the same she earned a few whistles.

The idea was that everybody should throw the dice three times. At the end of that, the articles of clothing would be returned after the forfeits had been paid.

Played while stone cold sober it was the kinda game that would have emptied a party. But with everybody steamed up on Atomic Bombs, they were just ripe for that kinda game.

Everybody, that is, except Dorothy Burden and Charles Skinner. You could tell right away they hadn't been drinking like the others. And you could tell right away this was a game they didn't wanna play. But then, they were two people who had more reason than most for not wanting to destroy Hugh Burden's idea of a good party.

The dice circled around. I was lucky. I threw a three and a one. I took off my jacket and squared the account. The dice-throwing went on around the circle and the disrobing continued. When it was Dorothy Burden's turn I saw her flush, and just for a moment she glanced at Burden. His black eyes were fixed upon her, sneering contemptuously. She bit her lip, shook and threw. She was an unlucky dame. She turned up two sixes.

There were a number of ways she could pay off. A dress rated 12, a skirt six and a blouse six.

Dorothy Burden was wearing a skirt and blouse. She looked at Hugh. And just for a moment I thought she was gonna fling out of the room. Then she bit her lip and took off her shoes.

That earned her two points. Everybody was laughing and calculating how she was gonna make up the 12 points. But she had it figured out. She unclipped her suspenders, rolled down her stockings. That gave her another two points, making four. Her cheeks were flaming when she fumbled modestly beneath her skirt. She fumbled for a long while, with a great deal of uneasy wriggling. Finally she worked a suspender girdle down her legs to the accompaniment of loud cheers. That earned her another two points, making six in all.

'Another six points, Dorothy,' called Burden, and his black eyes were gleaming wickedly.

'I'm aware of that!' she snapped. She slipped her blouse off her shoulders, and I realised why she had sacrificed her stockings and girdle instead of her skirt. She was wearing a brassiere and a slip. The slip was made of fine black georgette that was as transparent as a veil. Beneath it you could clearly see the tautly-drawn brassiere.

Dorothy earned herself quite a lot of admiring looks. But she wasn't in the mood to appreciate them. Her eyes were lowered shyly. Everyone looked at her and she seemed to be the only one who was uncomfortably conscious she was only partly dressed.

When the dice got around to the coloured maid she threw a ten. She giggled, rolled her eyes and said expressively: 'Ah'm gonna get around to it next throw for sure. Might as well settle now.' Her white linen dress buttoned all the way down the front. She shrugged it off her shoulders like it was an overcoat, and the whistles were really appreciative then because she wore nothing beneath that dress except a triangle of white material tied around her loins like a G-string. Her haunches were starkly revealed.

She got a lot of applause from the men. and some of the dames began to look mean. When the dice started throwing for the second time round you could see some of the dames were hoping to throw high numbers and give competition to the coloured girl.

By the time the dice cup worked its way to me again, most of the dames were in their undies and lots of the guys had lost their shirts. There were many showing bare thighs and bare chests and excitement was soaring high. I rolled and scored the best yet. Double one. I grinned, took off my shoes and passed the dice to the next guy in line.

There were lots of sixes and sevens being thrown. But it must have been Dorothy Burden's unlucky day.

She threw another double six!

Her cheeks were crimson as she looked at the dice. She stared at them for a long while. So long that nobody thought she was gonna move.

Hugh Burden spoke then in a voice that reached everybody clearly. 'It's 12, Dorothy. You've got to account for 12.'

She looked at him and the hatred was burning in her eyes. Then she fumbled at her side, let her skirt slip around her ankles and stepped out of it.

Beneath the slip she was wearing black, frilly panties. They were made of some airy-fairy material and you could see her skin gleaming through them.

'Still more, Dorothy,' said Burden. His voice was soft and gentle. But his eyes were hard and menacing.

Dorothy fumbled behind her, released the fastenings of her brassiere. When she pulled it clear, through the transparent slip you could see her breasts standing out taut and firm. There were many whistles of admiration and one or two of the guys gave wolf-whistles.

Dorothy had been unlucky. She'd thrown two double sixes. It had cost her a lot of clothing. Moreover, she had the disadvantage of wearing that transparent slip. Apart from the coloured girl, she was the only dame showing more than a swimsuit would show. And she came in for most of the ogling.

The trouble was, the other dames were Atomised and in the mood for this kinda thing, whereas Dorothy was stone cold sober.

44

The coloured girl missed her throw. A clause in the game stipulated that anyone unlucky enough to lose all their clothing might retain a minimum of one garment. The coloured girl had kicked off her shoes, and since she now wore only that white G-string she had nothing else to lose.

The dice started circulating for the third time. By this time the dames were so incensed by the attention Dorothy and the coloured girl were getting they were falling over themselves to get attention diverted back to them. By the time the dice got around to me there were as many bare-chested dames as there were bare-chested guys. There was an entertaining display of frothy underclothing and sleek thighs to go with them.

It really was my lucky day. I threw two more singles. I took off my shirt, which rated four, because I was hot, anyway. As long as I was able to retain my trousers I was happy. One of the guys there had got a laugh when he stripped off his trousers to show mauve-striped underpants!

By this time there was so much laughter, ogling, slapping and joking that Dorothy had dropped out of notice. She plummeted back into the public's eye very quickly, however, by throwing for the third time in succession a double six.

She stared at it as though hypnotised. 'It can't be!' she protested. 'It can't be!'

There was a sudden tense silence as everybody looked at Dorothy expectantly. This was the last time round, and while most of the folk there were showing something, none of them would be quite so low down the scale as Dorothy. Everybody knew that georgette slip of hers rated nine points. Then, after that, she'd have left only the single garment that she was entitled to retain.

But we could see through the slip that her panties were made of the same material as the slip, and once the slip was removed …

I guess Dorothy had it all figured out as well. 'I can't do it,' she protested. She looked around appealingly.

They laughed at her, encouragingly. Said she'd have to do it, said that it was all part of the game.

There was so much going on I didn't notice Hugh Burden until I saw him standing just behind her. There was a grim smile lurking around his face as he said clearly:

'Twelve points to make up, Dorothy.'

'I can't, Hugh,' she appealed. 'You know how I feel about these things.'

They were calling to her: 'Come on, Dorothy. Twelve points to pay. Peel it off.'

She turned back to them appealingly. 'Please!' she pleaded. 'Not now.'

Hugh Burden's action was so swift I hardly realised what he was doing until it was all over. He stepped up close behind her, pulled both her arms up behind her back, held them there with one hand while with the other he jerked the slender strap of her slip down over her shoulders. He cupped her right breast in his hand, pulled it from its scanty covering, and said loudly and cruelly: 'Here she comes, folks. Watch the last veil slip.'

He was baring her other side now, and she was screaming a protest. I'd been drinking too much. My reactions were slowed down. Everyone was shrieking with laughter by the time I got moving, and by that time Dorothy's slip was sliding over her hips.

I might have been slow off the mark. But there was

one guy who hadn't been drinking. That guy was Charles Skinner. And quiet, tall, thin guy that he was, he couldn't stand by and see Hugh Burden behave that way.

He got to Burden first, tore him away from Dorothy and gave him a shove that sent him staggering back a coupla paces. Dorothy slipped down to the floor, trying to cover herself with her hands and crying at the same time.

But if Charles Skinner had been quick off the mark, he was like a tortoise compared with the jet propulsion of Burden.

I caught just a glimpse of Burden's maddened red eyes, his flushed and anger-contorted face, before he sprang at Skinner. There was the meaty sound of knuckles meeting flesh, and Skinner skated backwards on his heels a coupla yards before he hit the floor. His head and shoulders hit the carpet like he was trying to knock a hole through the floorboards.

Most guys would have been content with that. But not Hugh Burden.

He gave a fiendish, leopard-like spring. He hurled himself at Skinner full length. He hit Skinner like a diver hitting the water, and his fingers crooked like steel talons around Skinner's throat.

For just a second there was stunned, motionless silence, and then everybody was shouting. Mostly they were shouting to stop him.

A wedge of four guys went in together. By sheer brute force and weight of numbers they dragged Burden clear of Skinner. Dane was there levering desperately. He yelled to me: 'Give me a hand, will ya, Hank? This fella's crazy. He'll kill him.'

There were six of us holding down Burden. I

figured five could manage it quite nicely. I went to the cocktail cabinet, got the soda siphon and went back with it. I enjoyed myself. I gave it to Burden in the face, drummed it against his eyes so that he couldn't open them, and when his lips parted to yell, I switched my aim and filled his mouth.

They had to hold Burden for ten minutes before he'd cooled off sufficiently to be let loose. And, like the clever guy he was, he carried it off well.

'Okay, you fellas. You can let me up. I've worked it off now.' He grinned. 'I guess you guys know how to deal with me when I'm blowing my top.'

We let him up and he was grinning widely. Maybe he couldn't control his temper. But he did his best to make up for it in the eyes of his guests afterwards. He looked around for Skinner. A coupla guys had carried Skinner to a chair and cleaned him up a bit with water. His lips were still bleeding and he'd lost a tooth. He was white-faced, too. But he wasn't hurt all that bad. Dorothy was kneeling by the side of him, holding his hand and saying sweet, loving things to him. She was so worried about Charles she'd forgotten about the striptease. She'd just tied the slip around her waist anyhow.

Burden went over to Charles and his face was all anxiety and apology. 'Gee, Skinner,' he said. 'I sure have gotta apologise for that. I shouldn't have behaved that way. I guess I deserved to be knocked down. How are you, pal?'

Charles opened his mouth. There was a look in his eyes that suggested he was going to utter some home truths. But Dorothy took his hand quickly, pressed it meaningfully, and all he said was: 'Bit of a misunderstanding, Burden.'

'Sure it was,' said Burden heartily. 'And I'm real

sorry. Will ya forget it? After all, I didn't escape scot-free myself. He tenderly fingered his chin. There was just a slight trickle of blood from the corner or his mouth.

'Sure,' said Skinner. 'It's all over now.'

'That's the boy,' said Burden. He reached out and clasped Skinner's hand, pumping it up and down enthusiastically.

Stella came up alongside Burden, linked her arm in his. 'Naughty boy,' she chided. 'You might have got hurt.'

'Not me babe,' he assured her, patting her arm. 'Not me.'

'You're so strong,' she sighed, looking up into his face. 'Nobody could hurt you, could they, darling?'

'I guess not,' he said. He slipped his arm around her and steered her across to the settee in the corner. She was one of the lucky dames who'd thrown low numbers. She was still wearing everything except her skirt and blouse. When I glanced over in their corner five minutes later, it looked like she'd thrown another double six in the meantime.

It had been an unpleasant little interlude but it quickly blew over. Someone put on the radiogram again. The maids came round with more drinks and the basket of clothes was taken outside by a coupla guys and hidden somewhere. It seemed it was too young in the evening yet for forfeits to be made in payment for the return of the clothes.

Things were going with a swing now. They were jiving again, lights were being turned out in the corners by necking parties and another little group were trying out acrobatics, balancing on each other's shoulders.

A hand tugged at my arm and a soft, husky voice said: 'Hello.'

'It's you again,' I said.

'Look what I found.' She was holding a gold fountain pen. But I wasn't looking at that. I was looking at her. She was wearing elastic-waisted briefs and a tightly-drawn hammock-for-two.

'I mean look at this,' she said, brandishing the gold fountain pen.

'Say,' I said. 'That's valuable. You find more of those things and you'll get real rich.'

'It's not mine,' she said. 'A fella dropped it.'

'What fella?'

'The one that got socked.'

'You mean Skinner?'

'Is that his name?' she said uninterestedly. 'What'll I do with it?'

'Give it to him back.'

'He's gone to the bathroom.'

'Shove it on the mantelpiece,' I said. 'I'll tell you when he comes back.'

'Come with me,' she suggested. She took my arm, steered me across to the mantelpiece. She put the pen on the mantelpiece, looked at my chest, impishly reached out and plucked one of my hairs.

'Hey,' I protested.

'I've been wanting to do that ever since you took your shirt off,' she confessed.

'Let's get a drink,' I suggested.

We drifted across to the bar. I poured some more Bourbon and we stood there chatting. I was keeping my eyes moving around. There was plenty to see!

There were a lot more folks dancing now. There seemed to be a lotta competition to dance with those dames who'd thrown the high numbers. The coloured maid had really let herself go now. She was dancing like a Dervish and her almost nude body was slick with perspiration. There were about three guys wanting to dance with her. But she kept slipping through their clutches. They seemed to like that. And from the way she rolled her eyes and showed her teeth in a wide grin, she seemed to like it, too.

Dane was sitting out with Pearl. She was wearing a pretty, satiny kinda petticoat, and it was cut so low in front you could tell she'd lost her brassiere in the game. It looked like they were hitting it off all the way along the line. They were just sitting there, her hand resting in his as they talked. Only occasionally now did Dane glance across towards Burden and Stella. You couldn't see much of Burden at that. He'd turned the lights off in that corner. But I knew and Dane knew that Stella was there with Burden.

Leslie Fuller recovered from the effects of his cocktail experiments. He climbed up from behind the bar just long enough to mix himself another drink. And then he slumped back into his position behind the bar, sitting with his knees under his chin and his head lolling on his shoulders.

The hand tugged at my arm again. 'Hey! You can look at me, too.'

I grinned into her black eyes. 'Sure,' I said. 'I'd like that.'

'What's your name, honey?'

'Hank. What's yours?'

'Lulu.'

'And what a Lulu!'

'What say we go places?' she suggested.

'Where, for example?'

She winked artfully. 'Some place alone where we can throw more dice.'

There came a loud roar from behind me. I spun around quickly. An argument had developed between two guys. They looked like quarrelling kids, because both were wearing their underpants and sock suspenders. But there was more than a childlike anger in their voices and demeanour. The row was over a dame. Both guys were wanting to dance with her. The expression on her face and the sulky look in her eyes indicated she didn't care which one she danced with and would probably like dancing with both. They were both pulling at her. Each had one of her wrists and each had an arm around her. She was wearing stockings and panties, and that was all. They way they were pulling her around it looked like pretty soon she might be wearing just the stockings.

Another dancing couple barged into them. One of the men pushed them away angrily and carelessly. His fist caught somebody's chin and it wasn't liked. And that was all that was needed. Ten seconds later, four of them were fighting it out, swinging mad, savage punches at each other while the dames screamed and dived in and out of the scrum trying to stop it.

It was what I had been expecting all the evening, and I sat back and watched to see how far it would go. A couple more guys joined in the fight and the struggling went on across the room and back again. Lots of the other folks stood back and watched, offering useful comments.

And then one guy went staggering backwards. His wildly out-swinging hands caught a large earthenware vase that stood on the mantelpiece. The vase fell on the hearth and smashed into a thousand pieces. I doubt if the guy even noticed what he'd done. He dived back into the scrum with blood streaming down his nose and the gleam of battle in his eyes.

But that vase was probably extremely valuable. It probably meant a great deal to Hugh Burden. His attention had been fully occupied elsewhere until now. But suddenly he was there in the struggle with them – a raging lion, the red glint in his eyes again and his face flushed and angered. This wasn't a fight any longer. This was a mad, outraged onslaught, with Burden slugging out all around with a killer's ferocity.

It took a dozen to hold Burden down this time. And by then the place was a shambles and lots of guys had smashed and bleeding faces.

When Hugh Burden had calmed down sufficiently to be released, the spirit had somehow gone out of the party. Folks were getting tired. The fight had an element of beastliness about it that left folks with a bad taste in their mouths. It was getting late, anyway.

The laundry basket was brought back and no forfeits were asked.

People sorted out their clothing, re-dressed themselves, and a kinda universal drift homewards began.

Dane came over to me with Pearl. He asked me if I'd seen Leslie Fuller.

Between us we fished Fuller up from behind the counter, thrust his head in cold water and got him conscious.

'He isn't fit to drive,' said Dane. 'I think I'd better take you home.'

'That's all right,' said Pearl. She gave him a soft, lingering look. 'I'll take Leslie home. The butler will put him to bed.'

'But how will you get home?'

'I'll borrow Leslie's car,' she said. 'He won't mind

that. Perhaps you'll help me get him out to the car?'

Dorothy and Charles Skinner was leaving, too. They both shook hands with me and went out to the car with Dane.

I rummaged through the laundry basket, found my shoes and sat down to put them on. There was a dame sitting next to me putting on a brassiere that was three sizes too small. She tried about six times to get herself manoeuvred into position, and when she didn't quite manage it she looked at me and giggled. I helped her out finally while she did a lot more giggling.

Nearly everybody had gone now. Dane came back, looked around, saw me and came over.

'Where's Stella?' he asked.

'Where's Burden?' I replied. 'Where he is, she'll be.'

'He's outside seeing them off,' he said. 'She must be in here somewhere.'

'Why bother?' I asked.

He didn't answer. Instead, he went across to the laundry basket, fished inside and came up with a green dress. Since everybody had gone home, and since everybody had got themselves dressed, it must have been the only garment left in the laundry basket. I saw right away what was in his mind. That green dress was the one Stella had been wearing that evening.

He looked around thoughtfully, went out. A hand plucked at my arm.

'Look, fella,' she said. 'He didn't take his pen. He's gone home without it.'

I looked at the mantelpiece. Charles Skinner's pen was still there.

'He'll come back for it,' I said. I wasn't worried about the damned pen. I was thinking of Dane. I had the uneasy feeling he was in the mood to do practically anything.

'Are you going to take me home, honey?' she drawled.

'Later,' I said absently. 'Just wait here, will ya, honey? I've got places to go.'

I followed Dane out of the lounge. All the ground-floor rooms were lighted. I went into all of them. Dane wasn't in any of them.

In a small room next to the kitchen the coloured maid who had been dancing was stretched out on a settee with a happy air of relaxation. Her eyes were closed, but her face was smiling and her white teeth gleaming. The fat man who'd been squashing grapes earlier that evening was sitting beside her. He was engrossed in plucking grapes from the fruit dish and crushing them between the girl's breasts. He wore an air of utmost concentration and the studied detachment of a scientist.

Somehow, the very look of that guy annoyed me. There was a large bunch of grapes in the bowl. I fished it out, went around him, put one hand firmly at the back of his neck and well and truly squashed the grapes into his face, into his ears and around his neck. I walked out, leaving him coughing and spluttering, and ran up to the first floor, the only place where Dane could have gone.

There was an alcove half-way up the stairs. A tall, broad-shouldered guy was struggling in there with another of the coloured maids. One of the maids who hadn't been drinking. She wasn't screaming but she was fighting him off with a kinda desperate fury. He'd got her dress open down the front and half over her shoulders. There was something impressive about the desperate silence in which she fought him.

Everything that had been going on all evening finally got under my skin. A guy can stand just so much. Beastliness had been mounting steadily in this house ever since I'd arrived. I had no idea who he was. But that didn't make any difference to the way I felt.

I took him by the collar, jerked him away from the girl, whirled him around, and, while he was still grasping in surprise, placed him carefully with the back of his heels on the top stair.

He was still looking surprised when I socked him on the point. I let him have it good and hard, with all the savageness of my outraged feelings. His shoulders hit the stairs half-way down and he turned a complete somersault before he hit bottom. When he hit bottom he just stayed there. I was beyond caring about him. I climbed the rest of the stairs and began opening all the doors I could find.

There were still some folks around. They were using darkened rooms.

I switched on the light just long enough to see what I wanted and then slammed the door on them.

The fifth door I came to was the one I wanted. I knew it, even before I opened the door.

I knew it because I could hear Stella. And Stella was as mad as hell. You could tell it by the high-pitched vibration of her voice.

Well, I was in the mood for trouble now. I'd just about got worked up to it. I seized the door-handle, twisted it savagely and flung open the door.

4

Stella was furious. Her tumbled auburn hair was gleaming like gold against her white shoulders. Her posture was arrogant and her eyes flashed. As soon as she saw me she said: 'You can get out, too!'

It was a bedroom. Stella was standing over by the bed and making a very pretty picture in pale blue, filmy underclothing. She'd been shouting at Dane, who stood at the foot of the bed, his cheeks flushed with anger and holding Stella's green dress in his hands.

I closed the door behind me and said quietly: 'Let's get going, Dane.'

He was mad but fighting hard to keep control of himself. 'I don't want no more trouble, Stella,' he said ominously. 'Put on this dress and I'll take you home.'

'For the last time,' she flared, 'I don't want you to take me home.'

'This ain't a nice place for you to be,' he said. 'I just wanna see you get home safe. There's a lotta wolves around with big ideas. All I want is to see you get home without any trouble. Now put the dress on and come along, will you?'

'Can't you get it into your thick head that I'm not

coming with you,' she flared.

'All right,' he flared back. 'So you don't want my company? Well, you can let Hank take you home. He'll see you get home safe.'

She looked at him, breathed hard and deliberately sat on the edge of the bed and began to peel off her stockings.

'What the hell are you up to?' roared Dane. 'You can't stop here!'

'And why not?' she demanded. She rolled her stockings into a ball, put them at the side of the bed and climbed in between the sheets.

'Stella,' pleaded Dane. 'Have you gone crazy or something? You can't stop here all night. Not in this house!'

I guess Dane sure thought a lot of Stella. I looked around the room quickly and formed my own conclusions. But Dane wasn't being very bright. Stella's hair was like a golden shower against the white pillowcase. The sheet was up beneath her chin and she was fumbling beneath it, working her body around.

'For heaven's sake, clear out, Dane!' she said wearily. 'If I want to stop here the night I will, and that's the end of it.'

'But you can't stop in this house,' said Dane. He was pleading with her now like he thought he could appeal to her affection for him. I could see right away she had no feelings for him whatsoever. He was a pain in the neck to her.

Her hand came up from beneath the sheets, holding dainty, frothy undergarments that she'd taken off. She dropped them on the chair by the side of the bed. 'Turn the light out when you go,' she said. 'I'm tired.'

Dane went almost frantic. He started trying to dominate her. 'I won't stand for it, Stella,' he said. 'Put this dress on now. And let me take you home. If you won't put it on –why, I'll make you put it on!'

Her eyes were murderous now, like knives. She reached one bare arm over the coverlet. 'All right,' she said. 'Give it to me.'

I don't know if Dane really thought she was gonna put the dress on. But he let her take it from him and then he just watched in a kinda shocked surprise as, relentlessly and deliberately, she destroyed the frock. She ripped at it, tore it into pieces and then flung it in his face. 'Now will you get out!' she mouthed at him.

'Let's get going, Dane,' I said gently.

He made one last attempt. 'Stella,' he pleaded. 'Do you realise what stopping here means? You know the kinda guy Burden is. He's liable to come in here. You know the kinda guy he is. You wouldn't be safe here.'

There was a hint of perplexity in her contemptuous eyes. She looked at me, shrugged her shoulders and then looked back at Dane. 'Are you quite blind?' she asked brutally. 'Are you quite so blind?'

Dane gaped at her. He just didn't understand.

'Use your head,' she said savagely. 'Look around. Take the blinkers off.'

Dane looked around blankly, uncomprehending. He saw the hairbrushes on the dressing table, the shoe-trees underneath the wardrobe, the suits hanging in the wardrobe, and finally he got it.

'By God, Stella!' he said in a voice that was cracked by dreadful realisation. 'This is *his* bedroom!'

'What a smart boy you turned out to be,' she sneered. Then she glared at him again. 'Now get to hell out of here, will ya? You're driving me crazy.'

You'd have thought that would be enough for Dane. But it wasn't. I don't know even now if it was sheer blind anger, jealousy or possessiveness that prompted him. But he moved in on her quickly, and there was desperate determination in his manner.

'You're coming out of here if I have to knock you cold first,' he gritted.

He pulled her half out of the bed before she bit his wrist. He slapped her face hard, and while she was still suffering from the shock of it he picked her up in his arms. She fought him, twisted away from him, kneed him savagely in the groin and tore his face with long fingernails. He kicked her legs from beneath her so she went down on her knees, and as she scrambled away from him across the room, he seized her thick hair, dragging her backwards, so that her body arched and she screamed aloud with the pain of it.

She made a nice study, bent back that way – firm, feminine curves and subtle hollows displayed to their best advantage

But this wasn't the time to take out a season ticket for the art gallery. Dane just didn't know what he was doing. And this kinda situation could lead anywhere. Especially if Burden came back.

I hated to do it, but Dane was my friend. I had no choice. His profile was in the right position as I stepped in close and swung hard. It was a swift, neat uppercut and Dane didn't even know it was on its way

His head snapped back on his shoulders, his jaw sagged and his knees buckled beneath him. I caught him beneath the armpits before his head hit the ground. I began to hoist him up again into a standing position. Stella was almost crying with vexation and annoyance. She went for Dane like he was still conscious, tried to kick him hard where it would hurt most.

I held Dane with one arm, reached out and shoved her away hard, the butt of my hand against her chin.

She flailed backwards until the back of her knees hit the edge of the bed.

Then she sprawled out like a jellyfish in the sun. She pushed herself up on her elbows, glared at me angrily and moved her jaws as though trying to make sure they would still work.

'I'm not Burden,' I told her bitterly. 'The show's wasted on me.'

She scowled, pulled the coverlet carelessly around her.

'Get that dope outta here, will ya?' she snarled. 'He's had that coming to him all evening.'

Dane was a broad-shouldered guy, pretty weighty. I got him over my shoulder, hoisted him off the ground.

'He asked for it and he got it,' I told her. 'You've been asking for it and you're gonna get it,' I warned. 'I guess Burden won't be long now. Then it'll be your turn.'

She sat there, snarling and spitting at me like a cat. I staggered across to the door, opened it and shut it carefully behind me. I found my way cautiously down the stairs and tripped over a guy lying at the bottom. He was the guy I'd socked. He was still out wide.

I got to the front door just as Burden was coming in.

'What's Dane been up to?' he demanded.

'Too much drink,' I said.

He chuckled. 'Never did like guys who couldn't hold it,' he said.

I hated that guy. I hated the way he talked, the way he swaggered, the way he grinned. I wanted to drop

Dane so I could take a poke at Burden instead. But my main job was to get Dane away from that house as quickly as possible.

'I'll be seeing you, fella,' said Burden.

'Yeah,' I said grimly. 'I'll be seeing you.' I looked him over in the kinda way that tells a guy you don't like him.

He sensed how I felt towards him. His hands clenched at his sides and his lips parted, showing his teeth. 'Anything on ya mind, fella?' His voice was aggressive, the stack of chips on his shoulder was a mile high.

'I'll be seeing you again,' I said. 'Besides, I can't detain you now. You've got company.' I jerked my thumb up the stairs.

He stood in the doorway watching me as I carried Dane across to my car. I couldn't see him but I could sense his eyes boring into my back.

I opened the door, wedged Dane in the back seat, and he stirred and moaned.

I wanted to get Dane so far away from there he wouldn't try going back.

I went around and climbed into the driving seat. A slight figure emerged out of the shadows, opened the door opposite me, and climbed in beside me. A hand reached out and clutched my arm.

'Hello,' she said.

'It's you again,' I grunted.

'You wanted me to wait, didn't you?' she said. 'You're taking me home?'

'That's right,' I said. I jerked my head towards the back seat. 'We've got company. He slipped up and banged his chin.'

By this time I'd got the car going down the

winding drive to the main drag.

'Is he hurt bad?'

'Not bad,' I said. 'He's just out for a while.'

'The poor dear,' she said. 'I'll see what I can do for him.'

Before I could stop her, she'd scrambled over the seat into the back. After that I could hear her slapping his wrists and talking baby-talk to him. As if that would help to bring him round!

I'd got maybe half a mile back towards Chicago when Dane recovered consciousness and got some idea of what was happening. He wrapped his fingers around my throat, squeezed so tightly I began to suffocate, and told me in a mean voice to stop.

I had to stop anyway. No guy can drive while he's being strangled.

And when I'd pulled in to the side of the road and jammed on my brakes I started wrestling to get his fingers away from my throat.

He let go abruptly. 'I only wanted to make you stop,' he said.

I caressed my neck tenderly. 'You could have asked,' I said.

'It's no good asking you to take me back?' he asked, in a voice that was strangely empty.

I turned around in my seat. 'Be a man, Dane,' I pleaded. 'There's nothing you can do about it. She wants it just the way it is. You can go back if you like. You can half kill Burden. Or he'll half kill you. But it won't alter anything. She wants it just the way it is. Tonight or some other night. Why don't you get it through your thick head that you don't mean a thing to her?'

He sat there in a strained silence. And even in the semi-darkness I could see how white his face was. There was a quiver in his voice when he said: 'I guess you're right at that, Hank. I guess there's nothing I can do.'

'I'll take you home,' I said gently 'You're all tied up inside now. It'll look different in the morning.'

He didn't answer. Instead he buried his face in his hands. He made a strange, soft kinda noise that coulda been a sob. Lulu said in a soft, sympathetic, understanding voice: 'Let's get him home, Hank. He'll be all right in the morning.'

A mile further along the road there were a coupla folk walking. I'd had trouble enough and I wasn't running a taxi service. I wouldn't have picked them up except that, as I passed, my headlights showed it was Dorothy Burden and Charles Skinner who were walking.

I jammed on my brakes and they came running up.

'Oh, it's you,' said Dorothy. 'You don't mind giving us a lift, do you?'

Charles Skinner hoisted himself in the back with Lulu and Dane, and Dorothy sat beside me.

'How are you feeling?' I asked.

'Wretched,' she said miserably. 'First he humiliated me and then he'd have killed Charles if the others hadn't stopped him.'

'Something will happen to that guy,' I prophesied. 'Someday somebody's gonna hire a thug to beat him up.'

She shivered. 'That's been tried,' she confessed 'The thug got the worst of it. He's so terribly strong.'

Charles leaned forward and said in his weak, ineffectual voice: 'I'll make him suffer for that! His deliberate humiliation of us. I can't let him get away with it!'

'Forget it,' I said. 'There's a lotta guys waiting to take care of him. Just give one of them time.'

I was thinking how perhaps that guy might be me.

I was thinking how perhaps I might bump into Hugh Burden some time, take that sock at him I was burning to give right now. It was a pleasant, warming thought as I drove along.

But the warming thought was driven away and replaced by a sudden cold dread feeling.

Dane lifted his head from his hands, leaned forward across the driving seat and asked in a hard, cold voice:

'Do you happen to have a gun?'

5

I pulled up outside a pleasant apartment block and Dorothy nudged my side meaningfully.

'Do come up for a moment, Mr Janson,' she said. 'Just look around. It won't take a moment.'

Charles Skinner got out of the car, too. All three of us walked to Dorothy's apartment. It was on the ground floor, overlooking the High Road. She opened the door with her key, switched on the light inside and beckoned us in.

'I'm worried,' she confessed. 'What did he have in mind when he asked about the gun?'

'Aw, don't take any notice of him,' I drawled. 'He's not himself tonight.'

'It's nothing to do with – Hugh?'

'Just a little trouble,' I said awkwardly. 'But he's been drinking too much. Don't take any notice of what he says.'

Charles Skinner said slowly: 'I can understand how he feels. I feel that way myself. Maybe, if I had a gun, I'd –'

'Don't be so melodramatic, Charles,' said Dorothy softly. She looked at him with gentle, loving eyes.

'A fella can stand just so much,' said Charles. 'But there's a breaking point, and –'

'You're a silly old dear,' she said, still smiling at him softly. She rumpled his hair. 'Run along now, darling,' she said. 'I'll see you tomorrow.'

I wasn't sure what the set-up was. I couldn't see that being unable to get a divorce from Burden meant Charles and Dorothy couldn't set up house together. But apparently it did. Charles kissed her goodnight, she shook hands with me and we drifted back to my car.

'Where shall I drop you?' I asked him.

'Don't bother,' he said. 'I don't live far from here. Just five minutes' walk.'

He said goodnight to us and then set off, his tall, thin figure disappearing into the shadows.

I went on from there to Dane's apartment. He was very quiet now. Very subdued. Yet I got the feeling he was seething inside. 'Will you be all right now?'

'Sure,' he said. 'I guess I'll take a shower before I hit the hay.'

'That's the stuff,' I said. 'See you in the morning.'

Going by car to a party has its disadvantages. Especially if it's a late party. You usually wind up acting as a taxi-driver for everybody and get home dead beat, hours after everyone else.

It was pretty late now. I had a full day's work ahead of me the next day. I was tired, and I remembered now that I'd concentrated on drinking all the evening and hadn't eaten a thing. I had that queer, weightless feeling in my belly that goes with drinking too much when you haven't eaten.

But I couldn't ditch Lulu. I had to get her home. When I pulled up outside her apartment block, she said: 'Come up and have a nightcap, Hank.'

'No, thanks,' I said. 'I'm hungry, I'm dead beat and I've gotta get up early.'

'I'll fix that,' she said. 'I've got a cold chicken in the ice-box. How does that sound?'

It sounded good. Real good. I went up. The electric clock on the kitchen wall said it was four o'clock. Just to look at it made me feel tired. Lulu opened up the ice-box, tore a coupla legs off a chicken she had. I snatched one leg from her and gnawed it ravenously.

'Coffee?'

'If it's black.'

As the pleasant, bitter aroma of brewing coffee began to fill the kitchen, I sat half on the edge of the kitchen table and chewed my chicken bone. She sat next to me, pressing her shoulder against mine. I stripped the bone clean, tossed it into the sink and fumbled in my pocket for a handkerchief to wipe my greasy fingers. Lulu already had her hand in my pocket.

'What the hell are you up to?' I asked.

She giggled, flashed her eyes at me and held up my key-ring, There were two keys. One for my car and the other for my apartment.

'What's this?' she asked archly.

I held out my hand.

'Give,' I said.

'Let me guess,' she mocked. 'Car key and door key. Right?'

'Right,' I said. 'Give.'

She giggled, moved quickly before I could stop her. Her hand lingered in the bodice of her dress and came away empty.

'What kinda gag is that?' I demanded.

She chuckled meaningfully, plucked at her waist. There was the soft thwack of snapped elastic.

'Don't let's play games, Lulu,' I said wearily. 'I'm tired. I wanna hit the hay.'

'Me too,' she said. 'When you're ready.'

'Jeepers,' I said tiredly. 'Don't start something. I'm not in the mood for a petting party.'

'I'm all right,' she said brightly. 'I feel fine.'

'Listen,' I said angrily. 'Are you gonna give me that key or have I gotta –' I broke off abruptly.

She nodded, smiled archly. 'That's right,' she said confidently. 'You've gotta get it yourself.'

I glared at her. Any other time I'd willingly have tangled with this dame. Twelve hours earlier I would have willingly tangled with her. But with the clock hands working their way around to five o'clock, I wasn't interested. I wouldn't be able to lie in bed until 12 o'clock next morning thinking how nice it had been. I had to work.

'I can handle that,' I said grimly. I swung off the kitchen table, went into the dining room and picked up the telephone. I dialled Dane's number. I was gonna ask him to give me pillow room on his settee.

She followed me curiously, stood there looking at me, a slightly worried look on her face. The lines connected and the telephone began to burr.

'Who are you ringing?'

'Friend of mine,' I said. 'He'll put me up tonight. Tomorrow I can get another apartment key if I don't come and twist that one from you first.'

'Why not do it now?' she asked.

'Because I'm tired. Because I've gotta get up in the morning. I told you that. Remember?'

It musta been a wrong number. There was no reply. I dialled again and got the same result. I kept the phone ringing so long that nobody, no matter how sleepy, could have endured it.

I hung up thoughtfully.

She smiled wickedly. 'Your friend's not home, then?'

'No,' I growled. I was wondering where the hell Dane had gone. I was remembering how he'd asked me about that gun. It was crazy. Dane wasn't the guy to get ideas like that. I dismissed it from my mind.

'There's nothing wrong with my bed,' she said. 'It's a feather mattress.'

I wanted to go home, shower, freshen up and get to bed. I'd seen too large a selection of boobies displayed that evening to have any scruples.

I twisted Lulu around, pulled her close and thrust my hand over her shoulder, deep down into her bodice. She giggled, wriggled, crossed her arms, pressed herself together and imprisoned my fingers. I kept fumbling and she kept wriggling and giggling. I didn't find the keys, but I found a whole lot of something else. I began to get all hot and bothered, and it wasn't on account of not being able to find the keys.

I began to get worried. I couldn't find the keys. She was squirming now, doubling up and giggling all the time. She was hugging onto my arm, imprisoning my hand like she was afraid I'd pull it away. But I'd set out to find those keys and I was determined to find them. I unbuttoned the front of her frock, pulled it down over her shoulders. She wriggled herself artfully, helping me, not resisting.

She kinda lay in my arms with the frock rumpled around her waist.

'That's nice, honey,' she crooned, as I loosed her halter.

I pushed her away from me angrily, went down on

my hands and knees and began searching the carpet. She was bare down to the waist and since I hadn't found the keys I figured they musta dropped on the floor.

Her voice was mocking. 'Can I help you, honey?'

I grunted.

She stood there, hands on hips, watching me with mocking eyes. She eased her dress down over her hips and stepped out of it.

I got up, red-faced, breathing heavily, and looked at her. 'What have you done with them?' I demanded hotly.

'Aw, honey, what do you trunk I've done with them?' she said, rolling her eyes.

Then her fingers strayed to the waistband of her briefs. She plucked. There was the soft thwack of snapping elastic, a sound that I'd heard before. I got it then. I knew where my keys were.

I was angry now. I said, 'Give – or I'll strip you!'

'Yes, please, honey,' she said quickly, working a husky, sexy tone into her voice.

I moved in. She moved fast, slipping around me, laughing and chuckling. 'You've gotta catch me first, naughty boy,' she cooed.

She was swift and slippery like quicksilver. We circled the dining-room table half a dozen times, knocked over a coupla chairs before she fled into the bedroom, screaming with laughter.

I finally caught up with her when she sprawled herself on the bed.

She was hooting with laughter as I grappled with her, she crossed her ankles, doubled her knees up beneath her chin and wrapped her arms around my neck. She thought it was great fun.

The way things were working out, it seemed Lulu

had had a lotta practice at stealing apartment keys this way. She seemed to know all the angles. Hugging herself together the way she was didn't give me a chance to get at those keys. I had to straighten her out first. And since she was as slippery as an eel and as wiry as a Japanese wrestler, the only way I could straighten her out and keep her straightened out long enough to get my keys was to sprawl my weight on top of her.

I was sweating for more reasons than one when I finally got the keys, and it was then she stopped giggling. She kinda relaxed, sighed, hugged me lightly and said: 'Hank, honey, you're wonderful!'

All this had taken time. I almost didn't waste that time. If it hadn't been for the clock in the living-room chiming five o'clock, I'd probably ... But the chiming chimes were like a cooling draught. I got up unsteadily, fumbled my way across the bedroom and to the door.

'Hank,' she cried. She propped herself up on her elbow and stared after me with angry, vexed eyes.

'Some other time, honey,' I said thickly. 'It's like I said. I'm tired. I've work in the morning.'

She came running after me, trying to pull me back, and she had the kinda curves to give her plenty of argument. But the magic moment had passed, shattered in fragments by the chiming of a clock. A clock that reminded me that in just a few hours I'd be sweating to make the deadline for the morning edition.

She was almost in tears when I left her at her apartment door. She couldn't very well follow me any further the way she was dressed – or undressed!

With a sigh of relief I got back into the driving seat, started the engine and pointed the bonnet towards home.

My homeward direction led me past Dorothy

Burden's apartment. As I've already said, it was on the ground floor. Quite naturally, I glanced at it as I passed. Then I jammed on my brakes and pulled into the side

The lights were full on, the door was wide open and lights were streaming out through the porch. I got the queer feeling there was something wrong.

I knocked on the open door and called. Nobody answered. There was that kinda quietness a place has when there's nobody around.

Cautiously I went in. I called again. I kept on calling. There was an open book and reading glasses by the side of an easy chair. It was as though somebody had been sitting there reading. I touched the chair cushions and they were still warm. I scratched my chin thoughtfully, walked across to what was obviously the bedroom door and pushed it open gingerly.

The room was empty. The bed hadn't been slept in. The kitchen and another room were also empty. I went back into the living room and looked at the easy chair and the book. Two and two made four. Dorothy Burden had been sitting there reading until a short time ago. Why should she go out suddenly at this time in the morning and leave the door wide open?

I shrugged my shoulders. I was getting less and less sleep. And there might be a perfectly reasonable explanation for all this, anyway.

I went back to my car, started up and steered down the road. Way up ahead was an all-night drug store. It was the only lighted shop front in the street. I saw somebody come out and come hurrying down the road towards me. It wasn't until I'd passed that I recognised it was Dorothy. By then there was no point in stopping. Everything was simple. She'd just popped out to the druggist to get something.

Just gone to the druggist to get something!

What did folks want from a druggist at five o'clock in the morning?

All kinds of thoughts whirled around in my mind. Burden. Poison. Murder!

It was crazy, of course. Dorothy seemed like a good, clean-living young woman. She wouldn't get crazy ideas. But then, all kinds of folks get crazy ideas. I slowed the car around and headed back. You don't burst in on a friend in the middle of the night and say: 'Have you just bought poison to murder your husband?'

I stopped outside the druggist, went in and put a five-dollar bill on the counter.

'What's that for?' he asked.

'The dame who just came in,' I said. 'What did she buy?'

He left the bill lying right where it was, looked at me, looked at the bill, and then looked back at me again: 'What's it to you, brother?'

'Don't get smart,' I warned. 'You know you have to put signatures in the poison book resister. I know who the dame was. Did she register?'

His eyes switched from me to the telephone. He edged a coupla paces sideways. 'Just what do you want?' he demanded.

'The dame who just came in,' I repeated grimly. 'What did she buy?'

'The nuts I get in here!' he sneered 'What d'you think a dame would buy in here at five o'clock in the morning?'

'I'm not thinking. I'm asking. Are you gonna talk, or am I gonna call a cop?'

He addressed an unseen audience. He gestured with his hands. 'What goes on in this town?' he asked them. 'Cops, poison books, dumb-faced guys demanding information. What kinda world is this, anyway?'

'You want I should come behind that counter and poke you?'

'Listen, bud,' he said grimly. 'Float! Take a powder! Scram! Get going before *I* call the cops.'

'Call the cops,' I challenged him. 'You can do some talking to them.'

'When I call the cops I have a reason,' he sneered. 'I don't call cops any time some half-baked tough guy wants to know why a dame orders a sleeping draught in the middle of the night!'

'Sleeping draught?' I echoed.

'What the hell did you think it was – arsenic?'

'Any poison in it?' I asked quickly.

His eyes looked at me keenly. 'Are you thinking that dame's a suicide case?'

'Why d'ya think I'm so het up?'

He flicked the five-spot with his finger so that it skimmed towards me over the counter. I caught it as it floated gently to the ground. 'Hold tight to your poke,' he said. 'She has a sleeping-draught made to doctor's prescription. I make up a bottle for her every month. You ain't got a thing to worry about.'

That took a whole load off my mind. It was after all a perfectly reasonable explanation. She'd been reading quietly at home and finally gone out to get her sleeping mixture. What could be more simple?

I got home at 5.30. I could hardly keep my eyes open. And just because there was a little worry still gnawing at the back of my mind, I dialled to Dane's apartment. There was still no reply. I hung up and scratched my chin thoughtfully. Probably, as in the case of Dorothy, there was some quite reasonable explanation for him not being at home.

I climbed out of my clothes, padded through to the bathroom, showered in cold water and then crawled into bed. I was dog-tired. I was asleep as soon as my head hit the pillow.

It was just half-past seven when the telephone began to ring and continued ringing incessantly. I swore, mumbled, clawed my way out through a sleepy mist and lifted the receiver off its hook. It was so pleasant when the jangling of the bell ceased that I just lay there with the earpiece to my ear, half slipping back into sleep.

And then slowly the frantic urgency of the voice began to probe into my consciousness. I sat up and said quickly, 'Give me that again!'

'You've got to come, Hank. It's terribly important. I'll go mad or something. You must come at once!'

'Stella!' I said. I breathed hard for a moment, and then: 'What's biting you?'

'There's no-one I could appeal to except you.' The desperate anxiety in her voice was coming over as clearly as though she was in the room with me. 'You must come over, Hank!'

'What's the trouble?'

'I daren't talk about it,' she almost whispered into the phone. 'I'm desperate – I don't know what to do.'

'Just how bad is this?' I asked gently.

'Terribly bad,' she said softly. 'Terribly, terribly bad.' There was a kinda choked horror in her voice.

I was gonna say, 'Why didn't you ring Dane instead of me?' wanting to be brutal to her, but checked myself, remembering Dane wasn't at home. I said soothingly, 'All right, Stella. Just sit tight. I'll be right over.'

'Don't waste a minute,' she pleaded. 'Not one single minute.'

I wondered what kinda trouble this was. I climbed into my clothes quickly and there was a dull ache jagging through my skull. Living at this rate, I probably wouldn't last more than another coupla years. I stopped long enough to rinse my mouth with Bourbon. My tongue felt like it was tarred and feathered. Then I went down to my car and drove over to Burden's house just about as fast as I could.

I guess I was still really half-asleep. Otherwise I might have guessed what I was gonna see when I got there.

Stella opened the door, dressed in her filmy underclothes. But there was a listless droop to her body and a haunted, frightened look on her face that dispelled any romantic ideas the underclothing might have given me.

She pulled me in quickly, closed the door behind me.

'What's this all about?' I demanded.

She pointed to the lounge. 'In there,' she said in a whisper. 'In there.'

I looked at the door of the lounge and then looked at her. There were black rings beneath her eyes, which were red and swollen like she'd been crying all night.

'What the hell goes on ...?'

'In there,' she said. She pointed and kinda edged back at the same time, as though there was something in the lounge that frightened her.

I guess I realised then what I was gonna see. I

walked carefully, pushed open the door of the lounge without touching the door-handle and stepped inside. The place was a shambles. Glasses, sandwiches, overturned furniture and the smell of stale tobacco. Just the way a place is after a hectic party.

And there, crumpled up in the middle of the floor, was Hugh Burden. He was lying on his back, one leg crumpled beneath him and his arms splayed out. His eyes were closed and his face was fixed in a wild grimace of pain. He was wearing only his pants, and that enabled me to see clearly why he didn't feel so good. The haft of a knife projected from between his ribs on the left side, just about where you'd expect his heart to be.

My mouth was dry. I licked my lips and moved over to him cautiously.

I found I was tiptoeing. I bent over carefully and touched him. There was a kinda unpleasant coldness about him. I knew right away he was dead.

I turned around, went back into the lobby. Stella was waiting there, plucking nervously at her frilly underclothing and looking at me like she thought I was gonna solve all the troubles in the world after a few moments' weighty consideration.

'Did you phone the cops?'

She shook her head. 'I wanted to see you first.'

'Why?' I asked bluntly

She put her hand to her mouth like she was on the point of crying.

'Dane,' she said. 'I thought …'

I knew what she thought. That thought was stirring around at the back of my mind, too. Except that Dane had been talking about a gun. I said tersely: 'What happened?'

Her lower lip was trembling. 'You've seen what

happened.'

'What d'ya know about it?' I asked wearily. 'How much of this did you see? When did it happen?'

'I don't know when it happened. I found him like it. I telephoned you immediately.'

'What were you doing before that?'

She shook her head, bit back a sob. Then she looked at me, trying to keep her lips from quivering. 'I don't know.'

She was upset, all ragged nerves. I steered her along gently. 'What time did Hugh Burden come up to bed last night?'

'Just after you left. But he went out again.'

'How long afterwards?'

'Almost at once.'

'D'you know what he went out for?'

She nodded. 'He said he was going to clear everybody off the premises. There were one or two drunks lying around. He said he'd leave them in the courtyard to cool off.'

'And then he came back?'

She shook her head tearfully. 'He didn't come back,' she sobbed.

I took her by the arm, guided her firmly into the next room and sat her down. I took her hands, looked into her eyes and said sternly: 'You've got to tell me what happened, Stella. I can't help unless I know what happened.'

I dragged it out of her bit by bit. She'd had a bad night, she'd had a bad shock and she was scared and badly hurt inside.

Burden had come up to the bedroom, made a coupla passes and then left her so he could clear out the one or two drunks that were still in the house.

She waited for him. I guess she'd been steamed up all evening and probably he seemed gone longer than he actually was. She decided to go look for him.

She found him. She found him in the little room next to the kitchen. Hugh Burden had done what he had set about doing. He'd cleared everybody right out. Everybody, that is, with the exception of the coloured maid. She was in the little room with Burden. What they were doing I didn't need to ask. At that point in her story, Stella sobbed on my shoulder uncontrollably.

Shocked, hurt and humiliated, she had run back to her room – or, rather, his room – locked the door and thrown herself on the bed. At some time later, Hugh Burden had come up, demanded to be let in the room, and threatened to break down the door. But she'd just lain there, crying loud enough for him to hear, and finally he'd gone away.

She'd lain there all night, sobbing bitterly, drinking down the bitter dregs of humiliation. And then she'd decided to get away from there as quickly as she could. It was early, but there would be taxis running. Her dress was in ribbons and unwearable. She'd crept down to the living-room to see if there was something she could wear lying around, perhaps even the coloured girl's dress. Instead, she found Burden.

'Is nobody else in the house now?' I asked.

She shook her head. 'If there had been, I guess they would have heard me when I first found Burden. I looked in all the rooms while I was waiting for you. It scared me. I was the only one in the house.'

'And you're worried about Dane?'

She looked at me with serious, thoughtful eyes. 'I was such a fool,' she said. 'How could I ever –'

'Write to Aunt Jane,' I interrupted rudely. 'She'll

solve all your heart problems. Why did you telephone me? Why didn't you get smart and run out?'

'Don't you think I would?' she asked. She looked down at herself. 'How far d'you think I'd have got dressed this way without attracting attention?'

'Yeah,' I said thoughtfully. 'That's right.' I got up.

'What are you going to do, Hank?'

'There's only one thing to do, Stella. You can't play games with a thing like this. It's serious. It's murder.'

'Murder!' She echoed the word, and her mouth was a wide 'O'.

'I'm gonna call the cops,' I said 'But don't worry. You'll be all right. Dane will be all right.'

I went through to the living-room, skirted Hugh Burden's body and dialled for the police. A quiet, efficient voice took down the name and the address. 'We'll be along in five minutes,' he said.

I went back to Stella. 'Remember this,' I warned her. 'You were scared when you found Burden. You didn't know what to do. So you rang me at once to get my advice. Understand?'

She nodded.

'A coupla other points,' I said. 'The last time you saw Burden was during the party last night. You were tired, you went up to his bedroom, locked the door and slept there. Sometime during the night you heard him trying to get in but you kept the door locked. Understand?'

She sat and looked at me with wide eyes. 'Don't I say anything about him being downstairs with the coloured maid?'

'The last you saw of him,' I repeated heavily, 'was before you went upstairs and locked yourself in the bedroom. Understand?'

'Anything you say, Hank,' she said quietly.

'Well, don't forget,' I growled.

After a few moments she said doubtfully: 'Don't you think I should tell the truth, Hank? You know what the police are like. They like to know everything.'

I took her by the shoulders, looked into her eyes and said: 'Now listen to me carefully, Stella. You didn't kill this guy, did you? I know it and you know it. You just couldn't have done a thing like that, could you?'

She shook her head.

'You don't know what cops are like,' I went on. 'You tell them that tale about Burden and the coloured maid and they'll get ideas.'

Her eyes widened slightly.

'They'll begin to figure that a knife is a dame's weapon. They'll begin to figure that you're the only person in this house. They'll even begin to figure that you could have sidled up beside him, pressed your fingers against his ribs and then eased the blade through your fingers between his ribs.

There was horror in her eyes. 'They surely wouldn't think that!'

'When did you last see Hugh Burden?' I asked her.

She swallowed. 'Just before I went up to my bedroom,' she said.

'Stick to that, Stella,' I said. 'You didn't see him again until you found him stretched out there in the living-room.'

'I'll do what you say, Hank,' she said quietly.

'I'll just snoop around again while I'm waiting for the cops,' I said. 'You wait here.'

I went back into the living-room, walked in very carefully and looked around. If there had been any kind of a struggle between Burden and the person who had murdered him, you wouldn't have been able to tell, because the room was a shambles anyway. I allowed my eyes to roam around the room, looking at everything and hoping that perhaps I might see some little thing that would give me some kinda clue.

In the far distance I heard the approach of wailing cop sirens. I hadn't much time. I looked around again, very slowly, very carefully, scrutinising everything. It was all more or less just as I remembered seeing it last.

I looked around just once more. My eyes alighted for a third time on the mantelpiece, passed on and then swept back again. There was something about the mantelpiece that I had to remember. Something that was important.

The sirens wailed to a stop outside the house. I heard rough boots scraping the asphalt. Heavy fists pounded on the door and the door buzzer began to work overtime.

'I'll get it,' I called to Stella, and went through into the lobby. I was opening the door when the realisation hit me. It slid right off the edge of my brain into my thoughts with such a bang that, as I opened the door to a uniformed cop who said loudly 'What goes on?'; I replied automatically and excitedly, 'Fountain pen!'

He looked at me suspiciously. 'What are you talking about?'

'I was just thinking,' I said quickly. 'Straight through there. Room on your left. It's a clear case of murder.'

He flashed me a cunning glance, shouldered his way past and went into the living-room. Four other cops trampled through after him.

I went back to Stella. 'There'll just be a little questioning now,' I said gently. 'Then we'll be able to get some breakfast and you can rest for a time.'

But I wasn't reckoning on resting myself. I was remembering how Charles Skinner had gone home the previous night leaving his gold fountain pen on the mantelpiece. I was remembering how he'd said that if he had a gun he might kill Burden himself. I was remembering, too, all the reasons he had for killing Burden.

And what made everything click together into a nice, neat picture was the fact that although the fountain pen had been on the mantelpiece when Charles Skinner had left the night before, now there was no fountain pen there at all.

6

Detective-Inspector Sharp and his partner Conrad arrived a few minutes later.

I knew both of them and they knew me. They loved me like a millionaire loves an income-tax collector, and I trusted them as far as I could kick an elephant.

Sharp brought up dead when he saw me, and he seemed to probe me with his steely eyes as his face set hard.

'So it's you,' he said grimly.

'Yeah,' I said apprehensively. 'It's me.'

Conrad put his hands in his pockets, stretched his long legs and gently rocked from his toes to his heels. He looked at me with the same kinda hard look.

It was just my bad luck that Sharp happened to be on this case. He was the one guy down at Police Headquarters I didn't get along with. The last time I'd tangled with him, he'd tried to pin a murder rap on me.[1]

'We'll play it different this time,' said Sharp. 'A guy that gets himself mixed up in trouble the way you

---

[1] See *Sister, Don't Hate Me* by Hank Janson.

do deserves to be handled carefully.'

'Listen, Sharp,' I said grimly. 'Lay off me, will ya? Don't make me get tough.'

Stella was listening to all this, her eyes wide open with surprise. She just hadn't had as much experience as me with cops.

'Gets worried quick, don't he?' commented Conrad.

Sharp grinned. It wasn't a pleasant grin. 'We'll talk later, Janson,' he said. He said it like it was a threat. 'Meanwhile, just keep out of the way.'

The fingerprint men came, the photographers and the doctor. I guess they went through the usual routine of checking up thoroughly, putting a chalk-line around the body and checking the cigar-butts in the ash-tray.

But I didn't know anything about that. Me and Stella were pushed into the little room next to the kitchen, where we just sat looking at each other moodily. Stella was too scared to say anything and my head was aching intolerably. There was a uniformed cop just outside the door who grinned when I wanted to take a walk and chested me back into the room.

'Sorry, fella,' he said. 'You've gotta stay put for questioning, even if you bust.'

It was more than an hour later when Sharp and Conrad came in. By that time Burden had been taken to the morgue and the cops had all the information they could get.

Conrad draped his lanky form along the mantelpiece. Sharp stood in the middle of the room slowly stripping the cellophane from a cigar. Neither of them said anything. But they both stared at Stella. I knew their tactics. They were getting her worried.

They succeeded, too. Stella looked from one to the

other, moved uncomfortably, looked away guiltily and finally asked: 'Do I start talking now?'

They still stared at her steadily. They didn't answer. In about three minutes she was as jumpy as though she'd committed the murder herself.

'Don't keep staring at me like that!' she yelled suddenly, a quarter of the way towards being hysterical.

'Why didn't you get dressed before we came?' suddenly snapped Sharp. And his steely eyes were suddenly busy, probing into the secrets of her body, which were scantily concealed by her underclothing. Stella wasn't a self-conscious dame. But the way those two stared at her steadily, stripping her with their eyes, got her worried. She crossed her legs, put her hands across her breasts. 'My dress got torn,' she faltered.

'During the party, huh?'

She nodded. Her eyes flicked to me. I wouldn't look at her. Sharp turned his steely gaze towards me. 'That kinda party, huh?'

'Burden's kinda party,' I replied.

'Just the kinda party a swine like you would like,' sneered Sharp. 'Undressed women, dolled up, golden-haired boys with high-pitched voices. Just your line, Janson. Have you got any coke on you?'

He was deliberately trying to get under my skin and he very nearly succeeded. I got up slowly, ominously, my fists clenched at my sides.

Conrad said causally, just too casually: 'Funny how some of these newspaper guys always wanna use their fists. A guy can go down to Sing Sing a long while for socking a cop.'

Sharp moved in close, his steely eyes glittering but mocking. 'Take a poke, Janson,' he said. 'Try it out, fella. Take a poke.'

There were half a dozen cops trampling around that house. I'd get maybe just one good poke at Sharp. After that they'd half kill me. And on top of it I'd get a stretch in jail for assaulting the police.

I sat down, seething. But I kept my mouth shut and unclenched my hands.

'You don't provoke?' said Conrad.

'We'll get around to him later,' said Sharp. He turned back to Stella, probed her underclothing with his eyes and asked: 'You found him dead?'

She nodded.

'Why d'ya do it?' he stabbed at her.

'But I didn't,' she protested, suddenly scared. 'I didn't do it, I tell you. I was upstairs all the time.'

Sharp held up his hand, commanding her to silence. He nodded briefly to Conrad, who pulled out a notebook and pencil, and then said: 'Tell it just the way it happened, lady. Use your own words. Exactly the way it happened.'

She wasn't a good witness. She rambled all over the place. But with Sharp stabbing questions at her, keeping her to the point, she told the simple story just the way I wanted her to tell it.

'It still isn't very clear to me,' said Sharp ominously, 'why you telephoned this monkey before you phoned the police.' He indicated me with a jerk of his thumb.

'I was scared,' she said. 'I didn't know what to do. I thought of Hank. He knows about these kinda things. That's why I telephoned him.'

'And how did your dress get torn?'

I could see Dane being implicated. I said quickly, 'You've got to tell him everything, Stella. Tell him the truth. Tell him I tore it.'

Sharp rounded on me quickly, furiously. 'Keep your trap shut!' he said.

But Stella was smart enough to follow up. She flushed, wouldn't look at me. 'Hank got a little tight last night,' she said in a quiet voice. 'We had a bit of a struggle before I went upstairs. I guess that's how my dress got torn.'

Conrad said: 'D'ya want to charge him with assault, lady? Could get him five years for that.'

'No, no,' she said quickly. She turned to Conrad appealingly. 'Please don't do anything like that.'

'You liked having your dress torn?' Sharp stabbed at her.

She looked back at him, her hands fluttered nervously. 'Of course not,' she said. 'It was a nice dress.'

'You didn't like having the dress torn, because it was a nice dress, but you didn't object to the act of it being torn off you?'

She looked at him, she looked at me, and then she looked at him again.

'No,' she said in a whisper. 'It was nice. I was only pretending to get away.'

Sharp let a long breath hiss out through his teeth and I felt my belly sink as he turned his attention towards me.

'Now!' he said.

Conrad's sharp eyes had detected something. He went down on his knees, fumbled beneath the settee and came up with something white. It was a triangular piece of cloth with tapes attached.

'What the hell is this?' asked Conrad, looking at it seriously.

Stella burst into tears when she saw it. The last time I'd seen it, the coloured maid had been wearing it around her loins.

'It's a G-string,' snapped Sharp, sourly. Then his eyes switched to me. 'This the only dame you tried to strip last night?'

I bit my lip, kept quiet.

He glided in quickly, smashed his knuckles against my lips. 'Answer up, dope,' he growled.

I looked at him venomously, wiped the back of my hand across my lips, and it came away smeared with blood.

'Stella's the only dame,' I grunted.

'Too bad,' he drawled. 'Too bad. But don't worry, Janson. We'll get something on you sometime. What do you know about this business?'

I told him simply that I had gone home from the party, Stella had awakened me and I'd come along straight away. As soon as I had seen what had happened, I telephoned the police.

'You'd never seen Burden before last night?'

'No.'

'You didn't have any grudge against him?'

'No.'

He fitted his thumbs into the armholes of his waistcoat. 'Know anybody who would have a grudge against him?'

I looked at Stella, and there was worry in her eyes. She was thinking of Dane. 'Yeah,' I drawled. 'Burden had a fight with a guy last night, earlier in the evening that is. There was another fight later. These things happen at parties.'

'Who was the guy?'

'A fella named Skinner,' I said. 'Charles Skinner.'

I wasn't telling Sharp anything he couldn't find out anyway. As soon as he got around to questioning folks, the fight between Skinner and Burden was the first thing he would hear about.

'What was the fight about?'

'Burden was behaving badly to a dame. Charles Skinner remonstrated with him. Burden tried to knock his head off his shoulders.'

'Who was the dame?' snapped Sharp.

I hesitated. Only momentarily. But during that time Sharp's hard knuckles pounded my lips again. His face looked ugly and his eyes were like ice chips. 'Don't tamper with the law, Janson,' he warned. 'Answer up smart!'

I hated like hell sitting there taking it from him, but I hadn't any alternative. I spat blood onto my handkerchief, glared at him balefully and mumbled: 'Dorothy Burden.'

'What caused the fight?'

I told him. I told him in detail. His eyes glinted at me like he thought I was the cause of it all. 'Fine friends you've got, Janson,' he sneered.

'I told ya. I've never seen Burden before.'

Once again it was his knuckles on my lips. 'Don't try any smart back-answers, Janson,' he warned.

I kept my head down, clenched my fists and fought to keep myself under control. There was nothing I wanted more than to plant my fist right in the middle of his puss.

'I think we'll see Charles Skinner and Dorothy Burden,' said Sharp. 'Maybe we can wrap this up right away. Send a patrol wagon round for them now, will you, Conrad?'

While Conrad was gone, Stella asked if she might have some coffee. Sharp spoke to the uniformed cop on guard at the door. Conrad came back, took up his position facing Stella and began to finger her underclothing with his eyes. A little later the uniformed cop came back with three cups of coffee and some biscuits.

'I'd like some coffee, too,' I told Sharp.

He sneered. 'I guess you would,' he said. 'But you don't get any.'

It was quiet in that room while we waited for the patrol car to get back. And I'd have given anything for a cup of coffee myself. Instead, I had to watch Sharp, Conrad and Stella drink theirs, while the aroma of it was sweet in my nostrils. Stella would have given me half of hers, but Sharp prevented her.

'I'll even up with you sometime, Sharp,' I warned.

This time it was Conrad who went into action. His lanky form uncoiled from the mantelpiece and his knuckles exploded against the side of my jaw. 'You mustn't be rude to the police, Janson,' he said mildly. 'You've got to be polite.'

I'd taken so much already it was worthwhile taking a little more. I kept quiet after that. I just hoped they wouldn't carry on until I really did lose my temper.

They brought in Skinner and Dorothy. They lived near each other and they brought them in the same car. Dorothy looked pale and determined, and Skinner looked as he usually looked, gangling and nervous.

Sharp got them seated and then fixed Dorothy with his eyes. 'You know why you're here, Mrs Burden?'

She stared at him, licked her lips nervously. She said, suddenly anxious: 'It's Hugh, isn't it? Something's happened to him?'

'What makes you think that?' he asked artfully.

She caught herself quickly. She looked around. 'The police here,' she said. 'Bringing me along. I may not be living with him, but I'm his legal wife. What else am I to think?'

'Supposing something has happened to him?' said Sharp. He looked at her keenly. 'You don't seem over-worried about him.'

'Hugh and I didn't get along very well,' she said. Then she dropped her eyes. 'We've been apart for three years.'

'But friendly enough to come to his party last night, huh?'

'Yes,' she said quietly.

'Supposing I told you your husband was murdered last night?' said Sharp quickly.

He was watching Dorothy, watching for some sign of reaction. She disappointed him. She raised her eyes slowly to his and then asked softly: 'Is that what's happened?'

Charles Skinner displayed interest. He sat up in his chair, leaned forward and said with a kinda mild interest: 'You mean somebody's killed him?'

'Yeah,' said Sharp. 'Did you do it?'

Skinner stammered, his mouth opening five or six times before he managed to get the words out. 'Of course I didn't,' he protested.

Sharp had been watching him closely to see his reactions, but I'd been watching Dorothy. She glanced at Skinner and there was a strange, curious look in her eyes. She glanced away from him quickly as though she didn't want Sharp to see her looking at him.

'You had a fight with him,' rapped Sharp.

'Not exactly a fight,' pointed out Skinner. 'I remonstrated with him and he'd have killed me if he hadn't been stopped. He's an awfully strong man.'

'Was,' corrected Sharp.

He looked back to Dorothy. 'Would you mind telling me exactly what you did last night?'

'I'll do my best, Inspector,' she said.

'What d'you mean? Do your best? You know what happened, don't you?'

Her eyes widened. 'Do you have to know everything?'

Sharp pushed his face up close against hers so that she shrank away. 'If you leave out one little thing, you'll be bucking up against the law. The law's a mighty powerful thing, lady.'

'But,' her lip quivered. 'Everything?' Her eyes were worried, concerned.

'Are you trying to hide something?' probed Sharp.

'One's private life …' she began. She looked at Skinner, and for a moment I thought he was puzzled

'Maybe you'll understand,' she said hopefully. 'Maybe I'd better tell you.'

'You'd better,' said Sharp grimly.

Dorothy flashed a quick glance at Skinner and then looked back at the Inspector. Her face was clear and her eyes wide and innocent as she said: 'When we left the party last night we had to walk because we couldn't get a taxi.'

'We?'

'Charles and I,' she explained.

'Carry on.'

'Shortly afterwards, Mr Janson picked us up in his car. He took us back to town. He dropped me at my apartment and Charles went home. He lives just a little way from me. Mr Janson drove on. He had some other people with him.'

'Is that so?' said Sharp, glancing across at me.

'Don't take my word for it,' I said. 'There were a

coupla other people in the car, too. Ask them.'

'Don't worry,' he sneered. 'I won't take your word, I'm only checking. What happened next, Mrs Burden?'

She bit her lip. 'I'd rather not say.'

He breathed heavily. 'Maybe you don't know how serious this is, lady. This is murder. Maybe you wanted to get rid of this guy. Maybe you came back and slipped a knife in his ribs.'

Dorothy gave a gasp of horror. 'A knife!'

'You look like you could handle a knife,' said Sharp evilly.

I half got up off my chair. Conrad's fist slapped me down again. 'Keep out of this, wise guy,' he snarled.

Sharp gritted, 'If you don't wanna talk, lady, maybe we'd better take you down Headquarters. I guess we wouldn't have to dig deep to find a motive. Burden's a rich man. How much do you get now he's dead?'

Her face was white. But she had plenty of guts. 'You're behaving abominably, Inspector,' she protested. 'And your unwarrantable threats make it necessary for me to tell you what is only after all a purely private matter.'

'I don't care what you think, provided you talk,' snarled Sharp.

She gulped. 'All right,' she said, 'I'll tell you.' She looked at Charles. 'I'll have to tell him, Charles,' she said. Then, as the puzzled look drifted into Skinner's eyes again, she turned back to Sharp. 'Mr Skinner and I are very friendly,' she said. 'Extremely friendly. If my husband would have divorced me, we would have been married some time ago.'

'Spit it out, lady!' snapped Sharp, 'Spit it out!'

She gulped again. 'Charles only pretended to go home. He came back as soon as Mr Janson had gone off in his car.' She gulped once more. 'Charles and I spent the night together.'

Sharp glowered. His eyes flicked to Skinner. 'Is that right?' he barked.

Skinner nodded. 'Naturally Mrs Burden doesn't want it broadcast. But that's the way it was.'

I was getting it all now. Skinner had somehow worked up the courage to come back and stick that knife in between Burden's ribs. He'd noticed his fountain pen at the time, picked it up so there wouldn't be any questions asked about it. He didn't think Dorothy knew about it. But she'd guessed and she was trying to cover up for him. She was giving him a first-class alibi.

And Skinner was being clever enough to take advantage of it.

'How long did this guy stop with you?' demanded Sharp.

She flushed and dropped her eyes. 'Until early morning,' she said. 'He left early because we didn't want the neighbours to –' She broke off.

'You folks are all the same,' sneered Sharp. 'Just popping in and out of each other's beds. Just a lot of tom-cats.'

Skinner half rose off his chair. 'I resent that –' he began.

'Siddown!' roared Sharp, and Conrad thrust his hand against Skinner's face, pushing him back into the chair.

'What time did you leave her flat?' demanded Sharp.

Skinner thought. 'I got home at seven o'clock. It takes only minutes to get from Dorothy's apartment.'

'Which of you two is lying?' rapped Sharp.

'I – er – er –' faltered Skinner.

Dorothy could tell Sharp was bluffing. She said crisply: 'Neither of us is lying, Inspector. If necessary we'll give this evidence on oath. And I can't really see what more evidence you need. If we hadn't spent the night together you would have had less evidence still. But it still wouldn't have made us murderers, would it, Inspector?'

Sharp knew they had a watertight alibi. Only by accusing them of complicity in the murder could he get them on the stand. But there was no real reason why he should think them guilty, anyway.

Sure, Burden and Skinner had fought. But Burden was always fighting. All the cops knew that. Right down from the Police Commissioner to the humble patrol officer. Sharp had just been digging, trying to get somewhere. And he'd come up against a blank wall.

'You can go now,' growled Sharp surlily. 'But we ain't through yet. You'll be hearing more from us.'

'Why?' asked Skinner.

Sharp was merely trying to get them worried, 'Why?' he demanded. 'Because this is a murder. Because she's his wife. Because you wanna marry her. And because she'll get a fair slice of his dough.'

'I wouldn't be too sure of that, Inspector,' said Dorothy. 'Why not check up with the solicitors before you're so certain on that point?'

Sharp's mouth stayed open as he tried to say something. Then he covered his confusion by rasping angrily: 'Clear out, both of you! But don't think you're pulling any wool over my eyes.'

I said quietly: 'I shan't say anything about this, Dorothy. What's been said here is in confidence. I shan't print anything that's likely to cause you trouble.'

She looked at me gratefully. 'Thanks so much,

Hank.'

'If the story does happen to get around,' I said meaningfully, and looked at Sharp, 'it's because some guys have got bigger mouths than they've got brains.'

'I think that's quite evident,' she said quietly.

Sharp looked at her and then he looked at me. He wanted to knuckle my teeth again. But too much rough stuff in front of too many witnesses was unsafe. He contented himself with breathing hard.

'If you're bothered with reporters,' I said, 'get in touch with me. I'll give you my telephone number.' I fumbled in my pocket for paper.

'I can look it up in the book,' said Dorothy.

'No,' I insisted. 'I'll give it to you.' I found an old envelope, looked at Skinner and said: 'Lend me your fountain pen, will ya?'

He didn't hesitate. He pulled out his fountain pen.

As I scrawled my telephone number, I examined the pen. It was the identical one I'd seen the night before. There were his initials on it and part of the clip was broken away.

'Thanks,' I said, and gave it back to him. I gave Dorothy the telephone number.

When they'd gone, I looked at Sharp and grinned. 'You ain't getting very far, Sherlock,' I said.

'I'm learning all I wanna know,' he said. 'I'm learning quick.'

Somebody knocked at the door. Conrad went outside and there was a conference beyond the door. He came back, looked at Sharp and said: 'There's an early report through from the doctor.'

'What's he say?'

Conrad looked at me meaningfully.

Sharp sneered. 'There ain't nothing he can learn

that'll do him any good.'

'Burden wasn't killed instantly,' said Conrad. 'It was a painful wound and a crippling one. He probably wouldn't have had the strength to do much. He was probably only partly conscious, anyway. But he didn't die at once. He just lay there, slowly dying.'

'What does all that mean?' snapped Sharp.

'The doctor reckons he couldn't have been alive later than seven o'clock, but the actual death wound may have been inflicted as much as three hours before that.'

'He could have been killed any time between four and seven,' mused Sharp.

'You want me anymore, Sharp?' I interrupted.

'I want some more information,' he said. 'I want a complete list of the guests.'

I shrugged. 'I only knew one or two of them. I can't help you there.'

Stella said quietly: 'I know who they were. I helped Hugh work out the list. I can remember all of them.'

He looked at her keenly. 'You and the Burden guy were pretty close, huh?'

'I – er – we were friendly,' she finally got out.

'Sleeping in his bedroom, huh?'

'Er – yes.' She flushed and lowered her eyes.

'Sleeping in his bedroom. But you shut the guy out. Wouldn't let him in. You're a cheap enough lay. Why didn't you let him in? Wouldn't he come across with enough dough? Or had he done something to make you mad? So mad you'd have slipped a knife between his ribs.'

'Lay off her, Sharp,' I said. 'She's already told you. She had a tussle with me. That pulled her down. She just didn't feel like it when Burden got around to hammering at the door.'

His eyes sneered at me. 'Big, strong fella, ain't you? You lay a dame and she has to have a fortnight's convalescence, huh? What kinda dope d'ya think I am? Where did this tussle take place, huh? There were maybe 50 or more folk milling around down here. D'ya give public demonstrations as well?'

Stella's cheeks were burning hotly. She wouldn't look at anything except the floor. I took a chance and said quietly: 'We were in here, see. I locked the door. It was that kinda party. Anything could happen anywhere.'

Conrad fingered the triangular piece of white cloth. 'Yeah,' he said drily. 'Anything could have happened.'

Stella began to cry again.

'Let me get outta here,' I said. 'You've got all I can give you.'

'Stick around, Janson,' said Sharp. 'We'll be in touch with you.' He leered. 'You still may turn out to be an accomplice.'

'Come on, Stella,' I said quickly. 'Let's go.'

'The dame stays,' said Sharp. 'She's got work to do. I want that list.'

Stella looked at me appealingly.

I shrugged. 'It's no good, honey,' I said. 'You'll just have to stop I guess.' I opened the door and then turned around. Sharp and Conrad had moved in close to Stella. Conrad had his pencil poised.

'Watch out for yourself, Stella,' I warned. 'There's a cop outside here. If they get fresh, just scream your head off. I'll fix up for somebody to send you a dress around so you can leave.'

I shut the door behind me quickly before Sharp could get mad. They'd given me a rough time, but it didn't stop me from feeling jubilant.

Sharp was such a smart guy he was going to wade through 80 or so guests, checking them all up, finding out what each of them was doing. And he hadn't a clue.

Whereas, on the other hand, it was quite obvious to me who the murderer was. I sympathised with Skinner and understood why he had done it. But he had still committed murder. And that was a capital offence.

I climbed into my car with my brain burning. I was getting all kinds of ideas, and a scheme in my mind was forming a pattern. A pleasant pattern. A pattern that would drive the *Chronicle*'s sales sky-high and at the same time give Detective-Inspector Sharp an unpleasant time, assuming he didn't get demoted.

I drove straight from Burden's place to the apartment where I'd dropped Lulu the night before. I went up to her apartment, leaned my thumb on the bell-push and waited. I still had that splitting headache, my belly was queasy because I hadn't eaten and my lips were sore and puffed up.

But despite all these things I felt on top of the world. Never before had anything seemed so clean-cut and easy.

'Hello,' she said softly, and her hand took my arm and steered me through into the living-room.

7

She looked pretty in the morning with her hair rumpled and her dark eyes trying to blink away the sleep. 'You've come back, honey,' she said. There was a sexy throb in her voice and she looked at me in the kinda way that suggested she'd been dreaming I was in her arms and had awakened to find it was true.

'I want you, honey,' I said.

'That's nice,' she said, and her voice was like hot syrup. She looked me over sleepily but approvingly, and lazily scratched her thigh.

I tried not looking at her. Even though I had all those ideas burning in my mind, she was liable to distract me.

She was one of those dames with ultra-modern ideas on dress and clothing. She hadn't bothered to put on a negligee and was wearing just her nightie. It was the latest type. Blue, transparent georgette, and as short as a man's jacket. It just managed to keep her covered when she raised her arms above her head. And she was raising her arms above her head and yawning right then.

I took a grip on myself. 'This is business, Lulu,' I said. 'Serious business. You've gotta got dressed and come with me down to the office.'

'Aw, honey,' she protested. 'Can't we curl up together and get warm first of all?'

'Honey,' I said, 'you do what I want now, and I'll do what you want some time later. That's a promise.'

Her eyes sparkled. 'Promise?'

I nodded, 'Yeah. Promise.'

'Come and help me dress, then.'

I went across to the bedroom door, stood there while she fumbled in the wardrobe. The ache in my head was splitting my brain apart. I couldn't even enjoy watching her fitting frilly things around her supple limbs.

'I've gotta have some coffee,' I croaked. 'Where's the kitchen?'

'Aw, honey. I like you to watch me.'

'Later,' I said. I held my hand to my burning head. 'I've gotta have coffee.'

'Okay,' she conceded grudgingly. 'Help yourself. Round to your right. Have you forgotten already?'

'Hurry,' I said. 'It's important.'

I'd brewed some coffee by the time she got dressed. I sipped the coffee and she pivoted on one dainty foot, inviting my opinion of her dress.

It was a nice dress, flared skirt and drawn taut across her belly.

'Forget about that,' I said. 'You've got to give some evidence. Important evidence.'

Her eyes widened. 'Evidence? Police?'

'No,' I said. 'This isn't a police matter. This is for the paper. My paper.'

Her eyes were still wide. 'What kind of evidence?'

'Keep this under your hat,' I said. 'This is just between you and me. Now I want you to remember back. Last night Skinner fought Burden. You remember?'

She nodded.

'Skinner dropped his fountain pen. You picked it up. It was a gold fountain pen. You remember what it was like?'

She crinkled up her brow. 'It had the initials C S on it,' she said. 'The clip was broken, too.'

'That's the girl,' I said delightedly. 'You'd recognise it if you saw it again?'

'I guess so.'

'Now,' I said. 'You've got to help me here. I want you to be very thoughtful about it. Skinner had gone to the bathroom to clean up his face after being punched by Burden. You put the fountain pen on the mantelpiece. Right?'

She nodded. Her eyes were still wide.

'Later on, Skinner went home. After he'd gone, you pointed out to me that he'd left the fountain pen behind. Right?'

She nodded again.

'There's no doubt in your mind about that? He went home and left the fountain pen on the mantelpiece. Right?'

'I remember it all,' she said.

'That's fine,' I said. 'Now I want you to come to the *Chronicle* with me and repeat what you've just told me. Understand?'

'All right,' she said. 'I'll do it. I'll repeat it. Just the way you told me.'

'That's the idea,' I said.

'But …' she began doubtfully.

'No buts,' I interrupted. 'All you've gotta do is repeat all I've just told you. And you know that's true, don't you?'

She nodded.

I sighed thankfully. 'That's all then, honey. Now don't get your lines mixed.'

'You don't want me to say anything that isn't true, do you?'

'No,' I said. 'I want you to say just what you've just said. You know that's true. That's all I want you to say. That's important.'

'All right, Hank,' she said quietly. 'Do we come back here afterwards?'

'Did you ever manage to stop out of bed longer than three hours at a stretch?'

'Often,' she said. She smiled wickedly. 'But not from choice.'

I finished my coffee. 'Come on,' I growled. 'Let's get going.'

The office was in an uproar when we got there. The old man had been yelling all over for me. I steered Lulu across the newsroom, holding her arm, pushing her in front of me. She gave saucy looks at all the other guys there and was greeted by a chorus of whistles. She liked that. She squared her shoulders, thrust out her chest another two inches and rolled her hips.

'Cut that out,' I said grimly. 'We're here on business. Remember?'

I steered her into the Chief's office, carefully closed the door behind me.

He glanced up, frowning, and growled: 'What in hell is this about, Janson?'

'Meet Lulu,' I said. I steered her across to a chair by the side of him.

She sat there, smiling sweetly, with her legs

crossed, showing her knees and underskirt.

'Get this dame outta here, Janson!' he growled. 'I've gotta few things to say to you.'

'Hold it, Chief,' I said. 'Hold everything. This is gonna be the biggest thing you ever handled.'

I leaned over his desk, pressed buttons on his intercom. I got through to Dane, asked him to come down to the office.

The Chief's face was red, his cheeks puffed like he was full of air and about to burst. 'What in hell you doing, Janson?' he yelled. 'We've got three-quarters of an hour to make deadline and we haven't a thing ready. Get that dame out of here and get busy.'

I tipped my fedora off my forehead with my forefinger, sat on the edge of his desk and grinned at him. 'You're gonna thank me, Chief,' I said.

'Thank you! What for?' His fist pounded on the desk. 'You're driving me out of business.'

'Chief,' I said earnestly, 'this is a scoop to make all other scoops look like peanuts. This is a scoop that'll –'

Dane came in. 'What's biting you, Hank?' he began as he opened the door.

'Lock the door behind you,' I said.

He arched his eyebrows in perplexity. But he did what I told him. 'Burden's been murdered,' I said shortly.

Dane's face was unemotional as he walked across the room towards me, but the Chief leaned forward, suddenly interested, his blue eyes blazing in excitement. 'Hugh Burden?'

'That's the guy,' I said.

The Chief reached for the telephone.

'What are you doing?' I asked.

'What do you think I am doing?' he rapped.

'Clearing the front page for the spread.'

I knocked the telephone out of his hand. 'Just listen for five minutes, will you, dope?' I said. 'You won't want the whole front page, you'll want the whole paper! This is a real scoop!'

'Hank,' he said earnestly, 'if this is another of your wildcat schemes ...'

'Are you going to listen?' I asked.

He glared at me, relaxed, sat back in his chair and looped his thumbs in his pants suspenders. His blue eyes stared at me levelly. 'Okay, Janson,' he growled. 'Make it good.'

'Burden was murdered last night,' I said. 'A knife in his ribs. There were 80 people at the party and the number of guys that would like to kill Burden would make an army. Sharp's working on it, but he hasn't a clue.' I touched my lips tenderly. 'He's been working on me, too.'

'He's got good sense, that guy,' said the Chief.

'Sharp's just about the dumbest dick on the force. And the *Chronicle*'s just about the best paper there is to get the news.'

'You trying to sell me this paper?' demanded the Chief.

'I'm gonna sell it *for* you,' I said. 'We're gonna rocket the sales. We're gonna get people buying the *Chronicle* every day. They'll trample one another down in the rush to buy.'

'Nice work,' he jeered. 'What do you do? Wave a wand?'

I leaned forward across the table, emphasised everything I said with my forefinger. 'Burden's been murdered. That's big news. It happened just a few hours ago. The cops haven't a lead. They don't even know it

110

was somebody at the party who's guilty. They'll follow it up for weeks – and probably get nowhere.'

'How does that help us?'

'Because,' I said slowly, 'because the *Chronicle* knows right now who the murder is.'

Dane's face went white. He interjected suddenly: 'What are you talking about, Janson? How can you know?'

I looked at him steadily. 'I'll prove it in a minute,' I said. 'But first let me give you the idea. The idea that'll sell the *Chronicle*.'

The Chief glanced at his watch. 'You've been talking two minutes,' he said. 'You've got three minutes more.'

I talked quickly. 'The *Chronicle* announces the murder of Burden with all the details. At the same time, the *Chronicle* announces it knows the identity of the murderer.

'But the *Chronicle* also says it cannot prove the identity of the murderer. Net yet. But, to show good faith, the *Chronicle* has sealed the name of the murderer in a safety vault. If the police find the murderer and convict him, and if the name in the safety vault as given by the *Chronicle* is not the name of the real murderer, then the Chronicle will make a donation of two hundred grand to any charity the police care to name.'

'You're crazy,' muttered the Chief.

I ignored him. 'But, on the other hand,' I went on, 'the *Chronicle* states that it is going all out to get proof of the guilt of the murderer. If the *Chronicle* furnishes evidence of guilt to the police, then it is entitled to consider itself more capable than the police force and the most up-to-date and factual newspaper in Chicago today.'

Dane said nervously: 'What d'you mean about proof, Hank? How can you have proof that the police haven't got?'

The Chief leaned forward. There was a gleam of interest in his eyes. 'Hank,' he said, 'You really have got something there. If we could show up the police that way, produce evidence before they did and get the public interested, our sales would go up.'

'It's in the bag,' I told him. 'I *know* who committed the murder. I can prove it now. But we don't have to prove it now. We can string it out a bit. Every day we write up a little more. There's no point in putting the finger on the guy right now. Get the public good and steamed up so they're buying every copy as it comes off the press. That's the way to do it. And then, just at the right moment, we'll step in, produce our evidence and say we just discovered it.'

The Chief snapped his fingers. 'Janson,' he said, 'if this comes off, you'll earn yourself a bonus and a month's holiday.'

'It'll come off,' I said. 'It'll come off all right!'

'Can you prove this?' asked Dane. His voice sounded anxious.

'She can help me prove it,' I said, looking at Lulu. 'But we've gotta trust her.'

The Chief looked at her earnestly. 'Can we trust you?' he asked.

She nodded. 'Oh, sure! You can trust me.'

'How much does it take to trust you? A coupla thousand bucks?'

She smiled coyly, dropped her eyes and then gave me an up-and-under look. 'I've got money of my own,' she said artfully. 'But I kinda like Hank.'

The Chief glanced at me, and there was a glimmer

of amusement in his eyes. 'You mean you'd do anything to help Hank – just so long as he's real nice to you?'

'He is real nice,' she asserted. 'I just want him to stay that way.'

I gulped hard. I said quickly: 'Well, it's between us four then. It mustn't go any further.'

'I know what you're gonna say,' said Lulu quickly. 'You're gonna say that Charles Skinner murdered Burden.'

I gaped at her. 'How did you know?'

'I just put two and two together,' she said simply.

I shrugged at the Chief. 'She's in on it, anyway. We've just gotta rely on her keeping her mouth shut.'

I told them everything. The way the fight had started, the way Skinner had dropped his pen after the fight. The way he had gone home leaving his pen on the mantelpiece. Then I told them how I called back later at Dorothy's apartment and found it empty, the bed unslept in while she'd gone to the druggists for a sleeping draught. It was obvious she was covering up for Skinner.

And then Lulu told her part. Just the way I'd asked her to tell it. And that beyond a doubt proved that Skinner had been back in Burden's house that night.

'It's an open and shut case,' I finished.

'Everything seems fixed,' said the Chief.

Dane said quietly, 'He doesn't look a killer.'

'Killers don't usually look killers,' I pointed out. 'Otherwise people would be on their guard against them.'

The Chief reached for the phone. This time I didn't interfere. He gave instructions for the pages to be cleared and prepared for a new set-up.

He hung up looked at me and said: 'All right, get

going, Janson, headlines on the front page: *The Chronicle Challenges the Police.'*

'That's the stuff,' I said approvingly

'Put Burden on page two,' he said. '*Famous Playwright Stabbed*. Build it up big. Give it everything you've got. Make it sound genuine. Say a reward will be given to anyone who is able to give information that will help prove the guilt of the murderer. There'll be a ceremony this afternoon. Say the Editor of the paper himself will deposit the name of the murderer in the safety vault while watched by important police officials who have been requested to attend.'

I rubbed my hands with satisfaction. 'The biggest scoop of all time,' I said. I looked at Dane. He was white-faced, biting his lip. 'What the hell are you so gloomy about?' I asked.

'I had a bad night,' he said 'Didn't sleep much.' Then he suddenly burst out: 'All I can say is, it's rough on Skinner. If a guy could get away with killing Burden I reckon he's entitled to. Do we have to put the finger on him?'

'No,' I said levelly. 'We don't have to put the finger on him. But he can't get away with it, Dane. He's not the kinda guy to get away with it. It's gonna be on his conscience for the rest of his life. Right now we can do far more for Skinner than by keeping him in the clear. We can build up sympathy for Skinner and criticise Burden. When we finally put the finger on Skinner we can throw everything in his lap. He'll probably get manslaughter. Maybe with leniency he'd just get two years. And after that he'd come out, a free man, nothing on his conscience. He'd be able to face the world again without having a guilty secret.'

'Yeah,' said Dane doubtfully. 'I guess that's right.'

He didn't sound very convinced.

'By the way,' I said, 'where were you last night?'

'Jeepers, Hank,' said the Chief. 'Get going, will ya? Those machines downstairs are waiting. Get going, will ya?'

I made a dash for the door. Lulu came running after me. 'Wait for me, Hank,' she cried.

The Chief cleared his throat. 'Lulu,' he said, and his voice was soft and kindly. When she heard him call to her that way she stopped, turned around with a sickly, dreamy look in her eyes, and smiled at him. Momentarily she forgot about me.

The Chief cleared his throat again, worked some more soap into his voice and patted the chair next to him. 'Come and sit down, honey,' he said. 'Let's you and I have a little chat, huh?' He flashed me a quick look as though to say, *Get going, Hank, I'll look after her.*

I closed the door behind me, chuckling to myself. Dane came out with me.

'I'll cover the Burden story if you'll do the rest,' he offered.

'Thanks,' I said. 'That'll help a lot.'

One and a quarter hours later, I leaned back in my chair, mopped my forehead and took the first good breath I'd had since I'd started. Downstairs the machines were beginning to revolve, churning out the *Chronicle*'s challenge to the police. The challenge that would cost the *Chronicle* two hundred grand if it wasn't successful.

'Thanks, Dane,' I said. 'You helped out fine.'

'That's okay,' he said. His face was still white and there was a strange look in his eyes. He nodded towards the Chief's office and said: 'Better see how he's making out.'

I went across, opened the Chief's door. He was sitting there with a sickly look on his face. He was pressed back in his chair, looking nervous and anxious. Lulu was sitting as close to him as she could get her chair. Her voice rippled like a babbling brook. She was telling him about an operation she'd had. Judging by the way her clothes were rucked up, she was trying to show him, too.

He looked up at me thankfully, like a drowning man who's been thrown a lifebelt. 'Have you done it?'

I nodded.

He breathed a deep sigh of relief. 'Take the day off, Hank,' he said. 'See the young lady home. Get the little bitch out of here!'

He'd said the last sentence without thinking. She turned around to him quickly with a look of shocked surprise on her face, 'What was that, darling?'

He stammered: 'I said "Get the little witch a beer".'

'Oh,' she said. She smiled at him, reassured. 'Just for one moment I thought you said something horrid.'

'The Chief wouldn't do that,' I said. 'He wouldn't dream of it.'

'No,' he said, 'of course I wouldn't.'

She took my arm as we went out. She also said loudly enough for the Chief to hear: 'He's a nice man, isn't he? But he's not very romantic.'

The fellas in the newsroom watched me as I walked through with her. They were admiring and jeering at the same time. I wanted to be around in the office. All kinds of things were liable to break. I wanted to be in the thick of it. I didn't want to be trailing back to Lulu's flat and learning just how good her tactics were.

When we got outside she said: 'Let's take a taxi.'

'I've got a better idea,' I said. 'Let's go by subway. It's so long since I travelled by subway. You don't mind do you, honey?'

She did mind. She didn't like it one little bit. She looked at me reproachfully. But when she saw I was set on it she squeezed my arm and said: 'Of course not, honey. Anything you like.'

We got our tickets, went down on the platform and I was able to steer her into the wrong train. I kept her talking in animated conversation until we'd gone a good way in the wrong direction. When we came to an interchange station I pointed out my mistake. We got off the train and changed platforms. There were lots of folk around. We all pushed into the next train. I pushed Lulu in front of me. I did it carefully. I did it so carefully that when the doors began to close she was on the inside of the train and I was on the outside.

She stared at me unhappily through the glass as the train began to gather speed. I gestured with my shoulders and gave her a despairing look. As soon as the train had gone I raced off to another platform. You see, I'd taken the precaution of switching her onto yet another wrong train.

Thirty-five minutes later I was back in the office.

8

The *Chronicle* challenge edition hit the streets before I got back into the office. You'd have thought war had started the way folks were lining up to buy it.

We all had our hands full. Already the print order was increased by 20 percent, and we started pumping out an extra edition, varying the page set-up and plugging the challenge to the police.

The Chief was getting a lot of publicity himself. He'd gone down to the safe deposit to seal away the name of the murderer.

It hadn't all been easy. He'd been having a rough time. The DA and the Mayor had rung him personally after reading the *Chronicle*. And right now there was a barrage of movie cameras waiting to record on celluloid the sealing of the deposit box. A hurried arrangement had been made for him to say a few words over the radio network

I slipped downstairs to the staff room for a sandwich and a glass of beer. I saw Dane there, looking pale and propping up the bar with a glass of Bourbon in front of him.

'What's eating you?' I asked, taking the stool next

to him.

His hands were quivering when he raised the glass to his lips. 'Stop getting at me, Hank,' he said. 'I've just had a lotta strain, that's all. That trouble with Stella …'

'Yeah,' I said sympathetically. 'Dames cause lots of trouble. Sorry you had to feel so bad about it.'

'I should have wised up to her sooner,' he growled.

'How's your jaw?' I asked.

He rubbed his chin and grinned wryly. 'You pack a punch, fella!'

'I had to sock you,' I said. 'You just weren't in a mood to see sense.'

'Sure,' he agreed. 'You had to do it.'

'That reminds me. By the way, just where were you last night?'

He gave me a quick look and there was furtiveness in his eyes. 'What d'ya mean? Where d'ya think I was?'

'I rang last night,' I said quietly. 'I didn't get any reply.'

He shrugged. 'Maybe the phone was out of order. I was home all right.'

'I kept trying,' I told him. 'It couldn't have been the phone.'

'Maybe I didn't hear it,' he said. 'I was taking a shower.'

'I rang early in the morning,' I said. 'I rang not long after I left you and I rang a coupla hours later.'

'Musta been the phone,' he said. 'I was home all right.'

I looked at him steadily. 'You wouldn't kid me?'

He scowled. 'You don't believe me?'

I shrugged my shoulders. 'What's it matter, anyway? Skip it. You drinking any more of that Bourbon poison?'

'Yeah,' he said. 'Same again.'

He would have sat there and gloomed, not talking, if I'd let him. But I made him talk.

'They're churning them out,' I said, 'They're selling as quickly as we print.'

'I hope you're on a good thing, Hank,' he doubted.

'What d'ya mean? Of course it's a good thing! We're riding every other paper off the streets.'

He shook his head slowly. 'I'm not so sure about Skinner,' he said. He said it doubtfully. 'I don't know that the evidence you've got is enough to pin it on the guy.'

'It's obvious, isn't it?' I said. 'You couldn't want it clearer. You don't expect a flashlight photograph of him doing it, do you?'

He still looked doubtful. 'I've got a feeling about that guy, Hank,' he said. 'He doesn't look to me the kinda guy that would bump off anyone.'

'Nobody ever does,' I said. 'It'll be all right.'

'It'd better be,' he said. He looked at me meaningfully. 'For your sake.'

'What d'ya mean?'

'The *Chronicle* is backing two hundred grand on this slant. That's a lotta dough.'

'It's safe enough,' I said. 'Don't you worry about it.'

'Why should I worry? It's not my dough.'

I left him there, still moodily sipping Bourbon. By the time I left, there was a neat little row of empty glasses at his elbow. But I didn't pay much attention to it then. After all, he had woman trouble. He needed something to steady him up.

When I got back upstairs there was a little guy wandering around the corridor outside the newsroom, looking for something.

He caught sight of me and came rushing over like he'd found a friend he'd been searching for over the years.

'Mr Janson,' he said. 'I must see you, Mr Janson.'

He looked vaguely familiar. I eyed him curiously and wondered where I'd seen him before.

'I must see you,' he said. 'It's most urgent.'

'I'm pretty busy right now,' I said. 'Couldn't you write a letter or something?'

He took me by the arm, his fingers eager and strong. 'You remember me, don't you? You must remember me.'

I looked at him doubtfully. 'Well ...' I began.

'Last night,' he said. 'You must remember. The party. I'm Mr Burden's secretary.'

I remembered him then. The quiet little nondescript man who'd slipped out of the party.

'Sure, sure. I remember you,' I said. 'But you don't have to worry. Mr Burden never even noticed you'd left.'

'It's not that I want to see you about,' he said. He pulled a copy of the *Chronicle* from under his arm. 'It's this,' he said.

'What about it?'

He glanced through the first page, found the point he wanted. 'It says here a reward will be given to anyone who can give evidence to prove who the murderer is.'

'That's right. What about it?'

'I've got some very valuable evidence,' he said.

I looked at him, drew a deep breath and took him firmly by the arm. 'You and me are gonna have a little talk,' I said.

'That's why I wanted to see you,' he said. 'You helped me and so I want to help you.'

'You sure are gonna be useful,' I said.

I steered him into the newsroom. It was lunch-hour and there were only a few fellas around. I knew the Chief was doing his stuff down at the safe deposit and decided to use his office. I propelled the quiet little man rapidly across the office and into the Chief's room. I don't think anybody noticed us.

I locked the door behind us, sat him down and offered him a cigarette. He didn't smoke.

'Now,' I said, with satisfaction. 'Just what have you got to tell me?'

'I'm not really interested in the reward,' he said. 'It would be useful, of course.'

'Adequate remuneration will be made for any information you give us,' I assured him. 'I know you don't want paying for this, but you won't object if we insist, will you, Mr ...'

'Carter,' he said. 'Thomas Carter.'

'That's a nice name,' I said. I sat on the Chief's desk, hitched up my trousers. 'Now,' I said eagerly. 'Just what have you got for me?'

'I went back to Mr Burden's house last night,' he said. 'Or rather, early this morning.'

I leaned forward intently. 'Do you remember what time?'

'I got back about half-past six,' he said. 'There were one or two things I should have done last night so I got there early this morning. About half-past six.'

I began to sweat with excitement. I could tell from his expression he had something really informative.

'Mr Burden was in his study. He was working.' His eyes looked at me seriously. 'Writing, you know.'

I nodded. 'I assumed that.'

'He was very annoyed with me,' he said. 'Told me

to clear out. Told me to get another job.'

I clucked my tongue sympathetically. 'Not a very nice man, Burden, was he?'

A look of black hatred came into his eyes. The kind of hate you'd never expect to see in the face of such an insignificant little man. 'He was monster,' he said with surprising vehemence. 'He was a monster.'

'He kinda had that reputation,' I agreed.

'So I left,' said Mr Carter. 'I left right away.'

That was rather like a damp squib. 'Is that all?' I asked, disappointed.

'I'm just coming to it,' he said. 'As I went out of the house, I saw somebody going around the back. I wondered who it could be. I followed him. First of all he looked in the windows on the ground floor and then he tested the French windows at the back of the house. But they weren't open.'

'What time was this?'

'About ten to seven,' he said.

My heart began to flutter. I asked anxiously: 'Did you recognise the man?'

'That's what I came to tell you,' he said. 'I recognised him all right. It was that theatre critic, Mr Dane Morris. He works with you, I believe.'

My heart ceased fluttering, stopped doing anything at all for what seemed a thousand years. Then it began to beat again, slowly, heavily and painfully. I listened to it thumping while I tried to get my breath back. At last I managed to say, in a very weak voice: 'What did he say about it?'

Carter shrugged his shoulders. 'He didn't see me,' he said. 'I didn't bother him. It was no affair of mine. I just left him to it.'

I licked my lips. 'Listen, Mr Carter,' I said. 'Do you

happen to know if Burden was still alive when you left him?'

'I should hope he was,' he said brightly. 'I'd been with him just a few minutes before. He was good and alive then.'

He sat staring at me while I sat there with a dull sinking feeling in my belly. I was remembering the way Dane had asked if I had a gun, the way he had deliberately lied to me about not being at home, and now there was this. Dane actually on the scene of the crime just a few minutes before Burden died. It must have been a few minutes. The doctor figured he must have died around seven o'clock.

I was remembering other things, too. I was remembering the *Chronicle*'s challenge to the cops, the name of Skinner sealed in the safe deposit and the two hundred grand the *Chronicle* stood to lose if anything went wrong.

I tried to keep my belly from dropping down to my ankles, stood up and crossed to the door.

'Shall I come with you?' asked Carter.

'You'd better wait here,' I said. 'I'm gonna get Mr Dane Morris.'

'All right,' he said mildly. 'I'll wait'

I crossed through the newsroom, opened the door to the corridor and saw Sharp and Conrad walking along the corridor towards me.

I knew Sharp was all set for trouble. He'd be as mad as a hatter about that article in the *Chronicle*. Almost at the same time, I realised we actually had in the office the guy who could put the finger on Dane Morris. Right then, I couldn't think about anything except not giving Sharp a lead.

I turned back into the newsroom, ran across to the

Editor's office and locked the door behind me.

Carter looked at me with startled eyes. 'Something the matter?' he quavered.

I glanced around frantically. The Chief had a wardrobe in the corner of the room where he kept his coat and hat. It was small; little bigger a coffin.

'You've gotta hide,' I said to Carter. 'You've gotta get right out of sight. There's a coupla cops coming in here. You've gotta stay quiet, not make a sound. Understand?'

'But why …?' he began.

I was bundling him towards the wardrobe, opening the door and pushing him inside as he protested.

'Why should I be afraid of the police?' he managed to get out.

'Listen, dope,' I said, like I was trying to jam good sense into him. 'You're in a spot, see? I haven't had time to figure this out. We've gotta play for time.'

'But I haven't got anything to worry about.'

'That's what you think,' I said. 'Figure it this way, Carter. You were the last guy to see Burden alive. Those cops are just dying to put a noose round somebody's neck. Your neck will be as good as anyone's. They'll figure out 40 different ways you could have stuck a knife in Burden's ribs.'

His face suddenly went white. 'I – er – I'm –'

They were already knuckling at the frosted glass door of the Chief's office.

'Your life depends on it,' I said fiercely. 'Just stop in there and keep quiet.'

He eased back into the wardrobe. I shut the door, turned the key in the lock and put the key in my pocket. I wiped the sweat off my forehead, crossed to the office door, opened it so that Conrad and Sharp could burst in.

Sharp had the look of a mad dog. He glanced around like he was looking for something to tear to pieces. His eyes came back to me and he snarled wolfishly, 'Where's Healey?'

'He'll be back soon,' I said calmly, trying to stop my heart from sounding like a bass drum. 'Why don't you guys sit down politely if you wanna see him?'

'If I wanna see him!' snarled Sharp. 'I don't wanna see him. I just wanna tear him apart, that's all!'

'All in good time,' I said gently. 'What say you boys sit down and get your breath back?' I waved them to chairs, dived down in the Chief's bottom drawer and came up with a box of cigars. That eased the atmosphere.

'What do you want to see him about?' I asked them when we'd lit up.

Sharp narrowed his eyelids and tried to drill holes through me with his eyes. 'As if you don't know!' he sneered.

'He looks innocent,' said Conrad. 'You can bet he had nothing to do with that article. Probably all he did was write it. Of course, he may have made a suggestion or two.'

'When you come to think of it,' said Sharp grimly, 'it seems just like what this guy would do.'

They both sat there and stared at me venomously. I worked up a weak smile and said: 'You boys think too highly of me.'

'Just wait till I get through,' said Sharp grimly. 'You'll see just how highly we think of you. Just about as high as the gallows are.'

'You boys are such kidders,' I drawled.

Conrad suddenly shot at me: 'Is Dane around?'

My heart knocked at the wall of my chest. 'Dane?' I

asked, with a sickly smile.

'Dane Morris,' said Sharp firmly. 'Get him up here. We wanna talk with him.'

The name Skinner was locked away in the safety vault. If the *Chronicle* was gonna be saved from ridicule and the loss of two hundred grand, I'd have to have time to figure things out. I got another sickly smile. 'Dane Morris,' I said. 'Oh, he's not around.'

'What d'ya mean, he's not around?'

'He's out of town,' I said. 'Had a special assignment.'

'Where did he go?'

'I'm not sure,' I said vaguely. 'He went by air. Long trip. He's gonna be away a month.'

'That's what he thinks!' snarled Sharp.

'Look,' I said quickly, 'why don't you guys go back to your office? The Chief will be a long while yet. I'll get him to come around and see you. I promise. You won't have to wait here. He'll come around and see you.'

'We'll wait,' said Sharp. He settled himself back in his chair more squarely. Conrad put his feet up on the Chief's desk. They looked like they were content to wait for at least a week.

'You fellas are wasting your time,' I said weakly. 'He's gonna be an awful long time. He just phoned through. Said he'd been delayed ...'

The door opened and the Chief came in. His blue eyes looked at me, flicked to Sharp and then to Conrad. Neither of them got up.

Sharp waved his hand airily towards the desk and said: 'Sit down, Mr Healey. We're pleased to see you. Mr Janson here was just telling us how you telephoned you weren't coming.'

Healey shot me a quick, enquiring look. I frowned

at him to be cautious what he said.

'Been getting yourself a lotta publicity, Healey,' said Sharp in a nasty voice.

'Pictures on the newsreel, too,' chimed in Conrad.

The Chief came around the back of the desk, took off his jacket and hung it on the back of his chair. He sat down with his arms on the desk. He looked from Sharp to Conrad and then back to Sharp again.

'Getting quite a big shot,' went on Sharp. 'Throwing your weight around, solving mysteries, doing the cops' work for them.' He came out of his chair suddenly like a propelled bullet. His face was red with anger as he hammered on the desk. 'You've just about had it, Healey,' he yelled. 'You can't get away with it. Printing that stuff is gonna cause you plenty of grief.'

The Chief stared straight across the desk into his angry face. 'You give them those cigars, Janson?' he asked. His voice was brittle.

'Yeah,' I said. 'Just while they were waiting.'

'Take them away,' he said, and there was a snap in his voice. I moved the cigar box from where I'd left it on the desk.

Sharp wagged his finger under the Chief's nose. 'I'm gonna have your trousers taken down in public, Healey,' he threatened. 'You're gonna take the biggest beating any paper ever had.'

'Are you going to get out, or am I going to throw you out?' the Chief asked.

'I'd love you to try it,' said Sharp.

There was a nasty situation developing. I eased alongside Sharp, took him gently by the arm. 'This ain't gonna get you anywhere,' I said gently. 'What say you sit back down and talk this over?'

For once Conrad was on my side. 'Take it easy,

Sharp,' he said. 'Do what he says. We've gotta do this properly, remember?'

For just a moment it seemed like Sharp was gonna slam out at me and then take a poke at the Chief across the desk. But somehow he managed to get his temper under control. He eased back into his chair, face still angrily red and breathing hard.

'You're learning a little sense,' said the Chief.

'I'm gonna teach you plenty,' threatened Sharp. 'You know it's an offence to withhold information from the police? Vital information?'

'I guess I know the law,' said the Chief.

'You claim,' said Sharp, 'that you know the murderer of Burden.'

'That's right,' said the Chief cheerfully.

My guts heeled over. If the Chief only knew!

'You're withholding evidence from the police,' snapped Sharp. 'I wanna know what evidence you've got.'

'None,' said the Chief smoothly.

'Then you're gonna be charged with disseminating alarmist news. You know you can't go fooling the public that way and stay at liberty.'

'What I've said is factual,' said the Chief. 'We know who the murderer is. But we haven't any evidence to prove it. We're looking for the evidence right now.'

'You're withholding vital information from the police,' repeated Sharp. 'I'm gonna drag you down Headquarters for that.'

'You can't bluff me, Sharp,' said the Chief smoothly. 'Every man is innocent until he's proved guilty. We've got no right to say who that man is until we prove him guilty. We know he did it. When we prove it we'll give you his name.' He sneered. 'Then you'll be able to arrest him.'

Sharp breathed hard. 'So you're gonna play it the tough way?'

The Chief grinned confidently. 'We'll play it any way you like. But just don't try pushing me around. I've got a newspaper behind me. And a newspaper's a mighty weapon.' He looked at Conrad and looked at Sharp, and there was an ugly twist to his lips when he said: 'It might even mean we get a coupla cops put back on the beat.'

I thought Sharp really was gonna start something then.

But Conrad saved the situation again. He said tensely: 'For Christ's sake, Sharp. Remember what we agreed on. Cut it out, will ya?'

Sharp got himself under control. He looked at Conrad. 'Okay,' he said. 'So we don't lose our tempers. We save it for some time when we can really get tough.'

'Some time soon,' mused Conrad. He smiled like he had something up his sleeve.

'I'm a busy man,' said the Chief. 'If you two guys haven't anything better –'

'We wanna see Dane Morris,' said Conrad smoothly.

'Dane Morris?' The Chief's forehead puckered momentarily. 'Okay, he said. 'Go right ahead and see him.'

'Where is he?'

'Somewhere in the building, I guess.' The Chief began pushing buttons. He asked his secretary to find Dane and have him sent up.

When he was through, Conrad said gently: 'We heard he was out of town.'

'Nonsense!' said the Chief. 'Why, he was in this

office this morning. He's around somewhere.'

Conrad's eyes flicked to me. 'Mr Janson specifically told us he was out of town and wouldn't be back for a month.'

The Chief turned to me with a puzzled look. 'Are you kidding? What's he talking about?'

'Don't you remember, Chief?' I said desperately. 'You sent him away on a special job. Don't you remember? You must remember!'

The Chief put his hands to the sides of his head like he was gonna pull out his hair. 'Jeepers!' he said. 'Is everyone around here stark mad? What are you talking about, Janson? I never sent Morris anywhere.'

'Maybe he was fooling,' said Sharp gently.

'I'm certain Dane's not in the building,' I said desperately. 'I'm sure you sent him out, Chief.'

Right then I could picture Dane sitting at the bar downstairs, waiting for the message to summon him to the office. I began to sweat all over.

'Janson,' said the Chief softly, 'there's two of us here and one of us is out of our mind. Which is it, do you think?' He pushed his face right up close against mine. 'Is it me, or is it you' – he terminated the sentence with a terrifying roar – 'that's stark, raving mad?'

'I guess I made a mistake,' I said. I crossed over to the door and stood with my back to them. I was wondering if by some miracle I might be able to stop Dane from coming into the office.

We waited there, we waited there, and we waited there. Hope began to rise inside me. Then the intercom on the Chief's desk began to buzz. He switched it on and the voice of his secretary rang out clearly: 'We've searched the whole building, Mr Healey. Mr Morris isn't on the premises.'

'Are you positive?' he growled.

'We've checked everywhere, every floor. Everywhere possible.'

The Chief switched off, and this time when he looked at me there was speculation in his eyes.

Conrad grinned knowingly. He winked at Sharp. 'Fancy Morris not being around,' he said.

'He should be,' said the Chief. 'Don't understand it!'

'Don't worry,' said Sharp. 'He won't be around much longer.' There was a note of quiet satisfaction in his voice that made the Chief glance at him sharply.

'What are you getting at?' he asked.

Sharp made a tent of his fingers, looked at the ceiling and smiled gently. For the first time since he'd come into the office he looked happy. 'It's gonna be kinda tough on the *Chronicle*,' he said. 'One of their reporters committing murder. Especially since the *Chronicle* knew about it and refused to give information to the cops.' He shook his head in mock sadness. 'My, my! What will the readers think?'

The Chief's face grew red. 'Look, Sharp,' he said. 'If you think that Dane Morris has anything to do with it –' He broke off. He looked at me and licked his lips. His shoulders drooped. 'Okay,' he said, 'I guess you boys are smart. You kinda figure out the angles.'

Conrad got up lazily. 'That's what we cops are for,' he said, with satisfaction. 'We figure out the angles.' He added, meaningfully: 'All the angles.'

Sharp climbed to his feet, flicked the cigar-ash contemptuously on the Chief's desk. 'We'll be seeing you, Healey,' he said.

'In court,' said Conrad.

The Chief looked really despondent now. 'I'm

sorry you got so far,' he said. 'I was figuring on giving the boy a chance. You know how it is; you work with a guy …'

'Sure,' said Sharp, nodding. 'We know how it is. But it kinda makes you an accomplice, too.'

'They've got a paper at Sing Sing,' said Conrad. 'If your conduct's good for five years you'll maybe get a job on the staff.'

They pushed out, closing the door behind them. I stood staring after them, my heart like a piece of lead.

The Chief came up behind me, chuckled, dug me in the ribs. 'I guess I fooled 'em,' he said. 'They've got a wrong lead. I think I acted that well. Kidded them along fine.' He slapped me on the shoulder and chuckled again.

I turned around dismally, walked moodily across to the wardrobe. 'What's eating you, Hank?' demanded the Chief. 'Here we are, sitting on top of the finest scoop of all time and you've got a face like a yardstick.' He chuckled happily. 'Can you figure out them guys,' he said, 'chasing after Dane? Figuring him out to be the murderer?' He chuckled again. 'Boy!' he said. 'We've sure got them fooled.'

I had my hand in my pocket, gripping the key of the wardrobe and ready to open it up.

The office door burst open and Sharp's face appeared.

'Just one more thing, Healey,' he said. 'We're looking for a guy named Carter. He's Burden's secretary. Seems to have disappeared. The police invite your co-operation. We want a picture and description published.'

'Did he commit the murder, too?' asked the Chief.

Sharp snarled, 'Do you publish it or not?'

'Give it to Hendricks outside,' said the Chief. 'It'll

go in the edition.'

'Remember,' warned Sharp, 'we're watching you, Healey. We're gonna get you hog-tied every way we know how. You don't happen know anything about Carter, do you? Where he is?'

'Never even heard of the guy,' said Healey. 'Wanna pin a rap on me for concealing a suspect?'

'If I could, I would,' promised Sharp. 'Just give me the chance.'

He went out and I followed him across the room, locked the door behind him. The Chief watched in amazement. 'What's the idea?' he demanded.

It felt like there was a rope around my throat. I did my best. 'You've gotta brace yourself, Chief,' I said. 'You're gonna have a shock.'

'What the hell's biting you, Hank?'

'You'll see,' I said. 'You'll see. Just prepare yourself for a shock.' I went over to the wardrobe, opened it, and Carter came out. A nondescript guy and very, very frightened. His lips were quivering as he looked from me to the Chief.

'And who the hell is this?' demanded Healey.

'Take a grip on yourself, Chief,' I said.

'Who is it?' he roared.

I licked my lips. 'Carter,' I said. 'Carter.'

'And who the hell is Carter?'

'Thomas Carter,' I said. 'He's the secretary to Burden. He's the guy Sharp just warned you about.

The Chief stared at me bug-eyed before his eyes slipped to Carter. His blue eyes went heavenwards, his hands went to the sides of his head and this time he really did begin to tear his hair.

9

The Chief was breathing heavily, his hair was dishevelled, his necktie was undone and there were beads of perspiration on his forehead.

He said with iron filings grating in his voice: 'So that's what you saw, huh?'

Carter nodded. He still looked scared.

The Chief said hoarsely: 'So Burden was alive at ten minutes to seven, and you left Dane Morris there while Burden was alive?'

Carter nodded again. His eyes were frightened like those of a child being told a ghost story

The Chief looked at me and breathed hard. 'Skinner didn't need an alibi,' he breathed. 'Burden was still alive at the time Skinner claims he was home.'

'Skinner hasn't proved he was at home at seven o'clock,' I put in quickly.

He gave me a sharp took. 'Let's check that,' he said.

Five minutes later he was talking to Skinner. He worked an oily note into his voice and said ingratiatingly, 'I'm Mr Janson's editor, Mr Skinner. I just wanted to check a little point from you. It's not for publication, of course. Mr Janson has explained that you'd prefer discretion exercised regarding your actions last night. But I understand you arrived home at seven o'clock this morning. Could you substantiate that?'

He listened and his face grew longer and longer. Finally he said: 'Thank you very much, Mr Skinner. That's just what I wanted to know.' He hung up, rested his arms on the desk and his shoulders drooped like an accused man's after the jury has found him guilty.

My mouth went dry. 'What did he say?'

'Skinner arrived home at seven o'clock,' he said in a dull, monotonous voice. 'He arrived there at seven o'clock, just as his daily help arrived. The woman who cleans up his place and prepares his breakfast for him.'

'How long did she stop?' I asked quickly.

'She was there until the police called for Skinner.'

A heavy blanket of silence fell and you could hear the clock ticking on the wall like the slow dripping of eternity.

'Hank,' he said in a sepulchral voice, 'we're in real trouble. We're as good as concealing a vital witness right now. One of our reporters is the prize suspect for this murder. We've got two hundred grand saying we can prove the identity of the murderer and the sure knowledge that Skinner couldn't possibly have committed that murder. It would take half an hour to get from his home out to Burden's place. But he was right there in his own home just about the time that Burden was dying.'

I knew the bottom was dropping out of everything. There was only one thing I could do. 'Listen, Chief,' I said urgently. 'Take a week's vacation. Let me take over. I caused this trouble. I'll take the rap for it. I'll accept all responsibility.'

He shook his head slowly. 'No go, Hank,' he said. 'I'm in this with you. I backed you. I'm not edging out now. We're in this together.'

That was just like the Chief. He was a straight guy. He'd never let you down. Just for a few moments I felt good again, just knowing that there were guys like the Chief around. Then the dull hopelessness spread through me once more as I realised just what a spot I'd got us into.

Carter asked 'Should I go to the police, d'you think?'

I snapped my fingers. 'Wait a minute, Chief,' I said. 'I can see a bit of daylight. If we can find the murderer, prove conclusively he was the murderer before the police do, then we don't have to open the safe deposit. We just publish the facts, say we found the murderer and handed him over to the police. We can give his name and everything. Just as though it was the same guy who's name is in the safe deposit.'

'That's just what you're gonna do,' said the Chief. 'You're gonna prove the murderer did the crime. But you've gotta prove it before Sharp does. And you know what that means …'

I looked into his eyes and there was an icy finger at the base of my spine. 'You mean –'

'That's what I mean, Hank,' he said grimly. 'Dane Morris is your friend. He's my friend too. And you've got just about the toughest job you've ever had. Dane looks the most likely suspect. You've gotta go after him. You've gotta pin him down.'

'You don't think …?'

The Chief's face was hard. 'I don't think Dane's a murderer,' he said. 'But it's possible. We've gotta check that. And if he isn't a murderer, maybe he'll know something more than we do. There could only have been minutes involved.'

'I hate to think it,' I said. 'Dane's such a nice guy.'

His blue eyes were hard. 'He's got a long-standing motive for not liking Burden. Burden smashed his play without a doubt. There may be other reasons.'

I swallowed hard. I thought of Stella. I thought of Dane's voice the night before when he had said: '*Have you got a gun?*' I remembered, too, his telephone ringing unanswered in the middle of the night.

'We can make it easy for him,' I said. 'Burden asked for all he got.'

Carter got up uneasily. 'Perhaps I'd better go to the police, now,' he said.

'You've gotta find Dane,' said the Chief. 'Find him quickly. You've got to get to him before Sharp does. And if it is Dane' – his voice broke momentarily – 'then you've got to bring him in yourself, Hank. You've got to bring him in with the proof. And we've got to publish that proof, have it on the streets before he's charged down at Headquarters.'

Carter started moving towards the door.

'Where the hell are you going?' demanded the Chief.

Carter jumped nervously, spun around like a startled rabbit. 'I think I'd better go and see the police,' he said nervously. 'Tell them about Mr Morris.'

The Chief got up, came around his desk. 'Are you crazy?' he asked. 'Do you wanna get yourself fried?'

'No,' stammered Carter. 'But –'

I took him by the shoulder, swung him around to face me. 'They'll crucify you, Carter.' I said. 'They'll put you in that sweat-cell underneath the hot lights. They'll keep at you. They'll keep at you for hours. There'll be

140

lights boring into your eyes. You'll be longing for a long, cool drink. And all the time they'll be gunning those questions at you. Do you know what'll happen?'

His eyes were wide. 'What?'

'They'll make you confess,' I said. 'They'll get you to say all kinds of things, trying to trip you up, making you contradict yourself. Before you know where you are, they'll have you in the condemned cell. Do you want that to happen, Carter?'

'They couldn't do that –' began Carter, looking worried.

The Chief took him by the other shoulder, swung him round to face him. 'In 1936,' he said heavily, 'there were three men executed who were later found innocent. A year later there were two men mistakenly executed. There are hundreds of cases of mistaken identity every year. Hundreds of guys are still serving sentences for crimes they never committed. Are you out of your mind, Carter? You can't go to the police with a tale like that!'

I took his shoulder, swung him back to face me. 'Right now,' I said gently, 'there's a guy in gaol waiting to take the last walk. He never could have killed the guy they say he did. It was circumstantial evidence. The jury found him guilty!' I paused, and then added slowly: 'That man is gonna die for a crime he never committed. Do you wanna die that way, too, Carter?'

He licked his lips nervously. 'What shall I–?'

'We mustn't let Sharp get to him,' said the Chief. 'We've gotta get him hid out somewhere. We've gotta keep him out of sight until we've cleaned up this mess.'

Carter said faintly: 'I'm willing to do what you two gentlemen say. I'm sure you know best, and –'

'It ain't gonna be so easy,' I said. 'Sharp's looking for him. His face is plastered all over the news-sheets by now. Even the people in this office are liable to recognise him.'

'We can't keep him here,' said the Chief.

'How the hell are we gonna get him out?'

The Chief scratched his chin thoughtfully. 'If we could get him to my cabin out on South Bend, he'd be safe enough there for a time. He could lie low, not see anybody. If you could get him there, Hank, you could take him food from time to time. He'd be safe enough there.'

Carter said faintly: 'I don't want to go too far ...'

'Shuddup, will you?' growled the Chief. 'Can't you see we're thinking?'

Carter lapsed into silence. He looked from one to the other of us anxiously.

'If we were to get him a scarf and an overcoat,' I suggested, 'I could get him down to my car and run him out.'

'And run the risk of being seen with him? Don't you realise how serious this is, Hank? Having this guy here is bad enough. Hiding him out is worse. Being found hiding him out will ruin us.'

'We've gotta do it, Chief,' I said. 'We've gotta keep him out of the way until I get something on Dane. We just gotta figure out a way to get him to your cabin.'

The Chief scratched his chin, got up and paced the room, His blue eyes switched to the wardrobe, rested on it, and then began to shine. 'We're getting somewhere, Hank,' he said. 'Genius,' he muttered. 'That's what it is. Genius. I just can't help it. I get these ideas.'

'What the hell are you talking about?'

He pointed at the wardrobe. 'I don't like that around my office,' he said. 'I want it taken away.'

'For god's sake, Chief,' I said. 'This is no time for

furniture shifting!'

'That wardrobe is going out to South Bend. It's gonna look a whole lot better in my cabin there, than here.'

'Chief,' I said excitedly, 'you've hit it!'

Carter was much slower off the mark than either of us. He looked from me to the Chief and then back to me. His eyes were wondering.

'Carter,' I said sweetly, 'you're gonna take a little ride.'

'I don't wanna go too far …'

I edged him gently towards the wardrobe. 'It won't take too long. All you've gotta do is be quiet and patient. We'll have you there in no time.'

He was still protesting weakly when I bundled him into the wardrobe, closed the door on him and locked it.

'You'd better follow out there, Hank,' he said. 'See Carter's settled down, and then go after Dane. Whatever happens, you've gotta get Dane before Sharp gets him.'

'I'm keeping my fingers crossed,' I said anxiously.

The Chief thumbed buttons on his desk. He ordered one of the newspaper vans around to the front of the office and three porters grunted beneath the weight of the wardrobe, got it down in the elevator and into the van.

It was maybe 20 miles to the Chief's cabin out on South Bend. It was a quiet little place, well off the beaten track, small, compact, but with all modern conveniences. I supervised the unloading of the wardrobe, tipped the helpers and sent them back to the office.

Then I unlocked the wardrobe, let out Carter, and helped myself to a drink.

'You sure everything's gonna be all right?' he asked anxiously.

'Sure,' I said. 'All you've gotta do is sit tight. Don't look out of the windows and don't answer the door. Don't go out under any circumstances. There's everything you need here, including food.' I showed him the basket of provisions I'd brought along.

'I thought maybe I should go to the police ...' he said.

'Carter,' I said, breathing heavily, 'don't you see we're doing all we can for you? Do you wanna fry?'

'Nobody does,' he said. 'But –'

'Then just do what I say,' I said firmly. 'Just stay put. Don't move. Understand?'

He nodded dumbly.

'I'll ring you later,' I said. 'Just to see how things are going.'

I went back to my car and drove down to Chicago. On the way, I was going through in my mind all the places that Dane might be. I guessed Sharp would be doing the same thing. It was a race now. I had to get to Dane before Sharp did – or else.

10

I spent three hours looking for Dane, telephoning and calling in at places where he was likely to be, and even checking the airport reservations. I didn't get a lead anywhere.

I shoved nickels into a drugstore telephone and dialled the cabin out on South Bend.

I got the engaged signal. That surprised me. Carter shouldn't be telephoning anybody.

I dialled again. I still got the engaged signal. I frowned, kept on dialling, and finally got through to him.

'Who you been phoning?' I demanded.

'Who is that?' His voice was anxious, eager.

'Janson,' I said. 'Hank Janson.'

'I'm doing fine,' he said. 'Nice grub.'

'Who were you speaking to on the telephone?' I demanded.

'Telephone?' His voice was surprised.

'Your line was engaged,' I explained.

'There must be a mistake, Mr Janson,' he said. 'The telephone hasn't rung all the time. I haven't been speaking.'

'Okay,' I grumbled. 'But do what I say. Just stay put. Don't communicate with anybody. Understand?'

'I won't, Mr Janson,' he promised. 'You can rely on me.'

I contacted Stella. She was at home trying to sleep off the worries of the night before. She hadn't seen Dane. Hadn't heard from him.

I tried lots of other places. Finally I got good and fed up at not getting a lead. I turned off the main drag into a little tavern frequented by newspapermen.

It's the kinda thing that can happen. Search a whole city without a hope, and then drop in somewhere casually and you find what you want. Dane was there, sitting at the counter, staring moodily into a half-empty whisky glass.

'Hiya, Dane!' I said. I eased myself onto the stool beside him, rested my elbows on the counter and said quietly: 'Anything you wanna tell me, Dane?'

He looked at me from the corner of his eye. His face was flushed, his hand was trembling, and his eyes were bloodshot. He was a long way from being drunk, though. 'What are you getting at, Hank?'

'What say you and me go somewhere quiet? Have a little chat, huh?'

'We can talk here,' he growled.

'Okay, fella,' I said. I called for a drink, and when it was set down in front of me I said softly: 'A friend's got to help a guy out of trouble. Are you my friend?'

'What kinda trouble you in?'

'Not my trouble,' I said pointedly. 'Your trouble.'

He looked at me steadily, and his eyes were unfathomable. 'Why don't you speak out loud?'

'Where were you at seven o'clock this morning?' I asked.

He looked at me long and steadily, then he turned away and took a sip from his glass. 'You really wanna know?'

'I think I ought to,' I said quietly.

'Hugh Burden's house,' he said, and kept on looking at me steadily.

After a few moments I asked: 'That all you wanna say?'

He nodded. 'What d'ya want me to do? Sign a confession? Do you want I should oil the machinery so I take a one-way ride to the chair and save everyone a lot of trouble?'

'The guy who killed Burden hasn't a lot to worry about,' I said. 'Burden got what he asked for. There's good grounds for defence for incitement.'

'What's the odds on Skinner now?'

'He couldn't have done it,' I said. 'Some new evidence just turned up.'

'I kinda figured that,' he said.

'You held out on us, Dane,' I told him. 'You knew the kinda trouble we were running ourselves into. You just let us go ahead and do it.'

'A fella's gotta think of all kinds of things,' he said.

'You gotta play it differently now, Dane,' I said. 'Your best chance is to come to the office with me. You've gotta lay it on the line. Give the *Chronicle* the first stab at it. We can write it up so it makes it good for you. Give the *Chronicle* the first stab at it. Then we can go down town and see Sharp.'

'Are you crazy?' he asked. He looked at me steadily. 'What the hell are you talking about?'

'You've had a lotta strain,' I said. 'You've got a problem on your mind and it's too much for one guy to carry around. The Chief's a good guy. I'll string along, too. Together we'll get some place.'

He said slowly and softly: 'If you mean what I think you mean ...' His voice broke off. There were a coupla guys standing behind us. They'd appeared there suddenly. One of them said in a harsh voice:

'You're Dane Morris, aren't you?'

I turned around quickly. They were plainclothes men. Tall, eagle-eyed and ready for action.

'What if I am?' said Dane.

'You're wanted down at Headquarters.'

Dane looked at me. 'You know anything about this?'

'Yeah,' I said bitterly. 'Sharp came around the office some hours ago. He wanted you then.'

'Suppose I don't wanna come?' said Dane.

'We can take care of that,' said the dick. 'We've got an open warrant. Do you want we should take you officially, handcuffs and all? Or would you like to be good – come quietly?'

Dane flushed furiously. 'Don't you guys try to get tough with me,' he said ominously. 'I'm not going to be pushed around by any –'

'You can have it which way you like,' said one dick softly. 'Handcuffs or without.'

I was all slumped inside. This was it. Sharp had won. He'd got to Dane first. That kinda clinched things.

Dane said: 'You'd better come along, Hank. You know how these fellas are. I'd like to have someone around.'

'Okay,' I said wearily. 'I'll string along. Might as well see it through.'

We got a taxi outside. Went down to Headquarters. Neither of the dicks said anything on the way and Dane wasn't inclined to be talkative, either.

We checked with the desk sergeant at Headquarters and then we were steered through a maze of corridors to the Homicide Department and into Sharp's office.

I gave a little start of surprise when I saw Leslie Fuller, the playboy, waiting there together with Pearl Gibbons.

I heard Dane's gasp of surprise when he saw Pearl. She looked up at him with soft eyes and smiled bravely. Sharp glared at me and rasped: 'What the hell are you doing here?'

'I just came along for the ride.'

'Get out!' he said.

'You wanna see me?' said Dane levelly.

'What the hell do you think I've had you brought in for?'

'If you want me to talk, he stops,' he said. 'Otherwise I say nothing.'

Sharp looked savage. He showed his teeth, and red spots burned high up on his cheeks. He said nastily, 'If you must have your wet nurse, I suppose he can stop. Siddown, both of you!'

Leslie Fuller had been looking at me with his eyes puckered up, trying to remember. Finally he said: 'I remember now. You're that man that invented the cocktail. Jolly fine cocktail, too. You invented a cocktail and invented an awfully good name for it, too.'

'That's right,' I grinned. 'World's End. It follows the Atomic Bomb.'

'I wish I could do that,' he said, regretfully. 'I've never done anything useful.' He looked at Pearl and there was softness in his eyes. 'Pearl's trying to take me in hand, you know. We're going to get married and –'

Sharp smashed his fist on the desk. 'For Christ's

sake cut it out!' he yelled. 'You've said that every five minutes since you've been here. Don't you know any other words?'

Leslie Fuller looked at him indignantly. 'It's entirely unnecessary to adopt that attitude,' he said frigidly.

Sharp raised his eyes to the heavens, sighed deeply.

'Just why you got me down here?' asked Dane.

'Yeah,' said Sharp, and leaned forward across the desk. His eyes bored into Dane. 'Just what were you doing last night, fella?' he asked grimly.

Just momentarily Dane's eyes flicked towards Pearl. But his eyes were steady when he said: 'I'm just not telling anyone that, Sharp.'

Pearl was about to say something. Sharp stabbed his finger at her. 'Shuddup!' he roared.

Pearl bit her lip. She looked down at her lap.

Leslie Fuller said: 'I think I ought to be told something about this. Why is Pearl here?'

Sharp breathed hard. He said through his teeth: 'Mr Fuller, do you realise why you are here?'

'I'd like to know,' said Fuller. 'I'd like to know why Pearl's here, too.'

Sharp's voice was almost a hiss. 'You're here to answer questions, Fuller.' Then he suddenly roared: 'You don't ask me questions! I ask you!'

Dane asked: 'All right if I go now?'

'All right if you go!' sneered Sharp. 'What were you doing last night?'

Dane was quite cool now. He said levelly, 'That's one question I'm not answering, Sharp. As far as I am concerned, last night's a complete blank.'

The answer seemed to please Sharp. 'That suits

me,' he said. 'I'll just give you a few facts. Then I'll give you one more chance. Maybe you'll alter your mind.'

Fuller said: 'Yes, give us some facts. Let us know something.'

Pearl had her hands in her lap. She was looking down at them and her cheeks were flushed. She was wearing a short, pleated, white linen frock and she was far and away the prettiest piece of furniture in that room.

Sharp said slowly and deliberately, his words distinct so they seemed to fall on the table in front of him with a loud noise: 'Hugh Burden was killed last night. A knife was thrust in his ribs. There were fingerprints on that knife. Badly smudged but sufficiently clear to match.' He looked at Pearl and I saw she was biting her lips. He said, almost savagely: 'The fingerprints on that knife were those of Miss Gibbons.'

It was like a blow between the eyes for me. It kinda rocked me on my heels. And the awful splitting headache started all over. Leslie Fuller half jumped to his feet.

'That's nonsense!' he said. 'Why, Pearl wouldn't –'

'Shuddup!' roared Sharp, and banged his fist on the desk so hard it almost split.

Fuller sat back in his chair. Sharp resumed in a quieter voice: 'Miss Gibbons admits using that knife. She admits that her fingerprints could easily be on that knife. But she claims she used the knife earlier that evening.'

'Of course,' said Fuller. 'Pearl probably had to open a letter.'

'Had to open a letter!' sneered Sharp. He pushed his face across the desk towards Fuller. 'I'll tell you what she did with it. She'll tell you, too. She stuck it in Burden!'

Fuller got up, and this time his face was white and

set. He looked like he was gonna take a swing at Sharp. But Pearl reached out, touched his arm, and it had a magical effect upon him. He yielded to her gentle touch like a five-engined bomber answers to the gentle pressure on the joy-stick.

'It's true, Leslie,' she said. 'I did stick a knife in Burden. But not that way. It was during the party. I'd been dancing a lot. I was hot. I went into the library for a breath of air. Burden came in and – well, you know the game we were playing!'

'Striptease!' sneered Sharp. 'A lotta cheap pick-ups and pimps!'

She ignored him. 'I guess Burden got excited. He tried to make love to me and I wouldn't let him. Then he became persistent. So persistent I was fighting with him. I don't know quite how it happened but he forced me back across the table. There was a paper-knife there. I got hold of it. I had to keep him away somehow. I jabbed him.'

Leslie said, appalled: 'You didn't, Pearl! You couldn't have killed him.'

'I didn't kill him,' she said quietly. 'I just hurt him a little, I guess. Just enough to make him ease up. He left me alone after that.'

'What she says checks,' put in Sharp. 'The doctor reports a knife wound in Burden's thigh. Not deep, not serious, but painful. When Miss Gibbons told us this, we already had the doctor's report in our possession.'

Leslie was visibly relieved. 'For one moment, Pearl,' he said, 'I thought –' Then his face clouded. 'This fella Burden,' he said. 'Why didn't you tell me about him? I wouldn't allow him to try that kinda thing with you. Why didn't you tell me?'

She smiled at him sweetly. 'You were just a little

under the weather, darling,' she pointed out

He'd been under the counter, too! Flat out!

Sharp suddenly shot at Dane: 'Did you spend last night with Miss Gibbons?'

Dane looked startled. Then he said: 'What a helluva question! You want I should kick your teeth down your throat?'

'You want *I* should?' asked Leslie Fuller. He was quivering with rage now. 'How dare you make such a suggestion! Miss Gibbons is engaged to marry me.'

Sharp grinned evilly. 'Maybe she is, fella,' he said. 'But the folks at Burden's party weren't choosey kinda people.'

Fuller gritted his teeth. He said, 'That's an outrageous accusation. Miss Gibbons isn't the sort of girl to do that kind of thing. Why, yesterday was her first time in Chicago, and as for sleeping with Dane, she met him for the first time last night.'

Sharp looked at Dane steadily. 'Did you sleep with Miss Gibbons last night?' he asked. 'Can you alibi her? From after she left the party until early this morning?'

'No,' said Dane bluntly. 'I wasn't with Miss Gibbons.'

She gave a kinda sigh. He looked at her quickly. She said: 'I think you ought to tell them, Dane. It's better this way. We couldn't go on the way it was.'

'What are you talking about?' asked Leslie.

Dane looked at her steadily, and suddenly I saw something in their eyes, something that made me realise a whole lot of things.

Sharp said, 'I think you've cleared things up for us, Dane. A dame who can stab a knife into a guy while there's a party going on can easily slip back later and make a job of it. Miss Gibbons stated you were with her last night. You say you weren't. That kinda ties the thing up.' He looked at Pearl. 'I'll have to hold you, Miss Gibbons,' he said. 'We'll be charging you.'

'Just a minute,' said Fuller. 'You can't ...'

Pearl said: 'Please, Dane, it doesn't matter now. Everything's different. It's better to be honest.'

Dane looked at her steadily for a long while. Then he licked his lips. 'All right, Sharp,' he said. 'I was with her. We spent the night together.'

Fuller said: 'What the hell are you talking about? It isn't possible. You couldn't have done that!'

Dane rounded on him. 'You want to see her kept in jail?' he rasped. 'I'm giving her an alibi, aren't I? You want she should be charged with murder?'

Fuller looked like he didn't know what to think. 'Well – I – I guess I don't know.'

Sharp said gently and evilly: 'That was a kinda slick confession, Dane. Just a bit too slick. First you deny it, and then you admit it.'

'Of course I denied it!' said Dane. 'Pearl's engaged. She's going to marry Fuller. It was just something that happened. Do you think I want to spoil her life? I was gonna forget all about it, let her go ahead and marry Fuller.'

'Of all the confounded cheek!' said Fuller hotly. He was up on his feet again. It needed Pearl's gentle touch on his arm to get him sitting once more.

Sharp said: 'No dice, Morris. I'm keeping the dame. And I'm considering holding you for perjury. You can't cook up an alibi that easy.'

'Wait a minute!' said Pearl, Her cheeks were flushed and her face was set, but she was quite cool. 'I've never been to Chicago before,' she said. 'Lived in Florida all my life. I met Leslie in Florida six months ago. I came to Chicago yesterday with him and we're to be married in a month's time. That's right, Leslie?'

He nodded. There was a perplexed look in his eyes. 'Absolutely right,' he confirmed.

'And I met Mr Dane for the first time last night,' she said. 'I'd never seen him before. Is that right, Leslie?'

'It must be, I suppose,' he said.

She looked at Dane steadily. 'It doesn't matter now, Dane,' she said. 'Leslie will have to know. It's better this way. I couldn't have married him the way things were, anyway.'

Sharp said: 'What are you getting at? I'm slapping a charge on you. Is there anything you want to add before I do it?'

'That's just what I'm doing,' she said. 'I'm going to prove to you that Dane and I were together last night.'

'Sure,' grinned Sharp. 'You took Janson along with you to be a witness. He'll give you another alibi.'

She said quietly: 'Dane's never had any opportunity to see me other than last night.' She looked at Dane. 'Do you remember what particularly intrigued you last night?' There was a soft meaning in her eyes.

Dane stared back at her. He nodded slowly.

'Write it down on a piece of paper,' she said. 'Fold it up. Give it to the Inspector. Let him hold it.'

'You mean …?' said Dane.

She nodded. 'It'll make everything clear,' she said.

Dane took out his notebook, scribbled something on it, folded the sheet into quarters and handed it to Sharp.

Sharp looked puzzled, but interested. 'What about it?' he asked.

'I can't think of any other way to prove what we've been telling you,' Pearl said. 'You want the truth and proof and you'll have to have it.'

'What kinda ...'? began Sharp. Then his eyes widened and his mouth opened slowly.

Pearl stood up, gathered up the hem of her skirt, pulled it high around her waist, held it there with one arm. Her long slim legs were milky white and soft.

'You can't do that here!' yelled Sharp. 'Stop that, d'ya hear?'

'For heaven's sake!' she said quietly and wearily, and somehow her dry, unemotional attitude was that this was just a job that had to be done, got over. He sank back in his chair, eyes wide, mouth gaping.

She fumbled with her free hand at the buttons on her panties. There was the soft rustle of silk as they slipped through her fingers, revealing the taut, flat curve of her belly, and then whispered swiftly down around her ankles.

There was a kinda universal sigh of awe. Fuller was gaping like he couldn't believe his eyes. Dane was watching her unemotionally, and Sharp looked like he was having apoplexy.

There was a deep flush on Pearl's cheeks but a grim sparkle of determination in her eyes. She stepped out of the panties, angled around to face Sharp with her legs astride and then held herself in an unnatural position so he could see what she was indicating.

He stared, fascinated, his Adam's apple bobbing up and down like an imp in a bottle every time he swallowed. And he swallowed good and often. I thought he'd go on looking for the rest of his life.

'Have you seen it yet?' she asked with a light, controlled voice.

'Yeah,' he said. 'I've seen it.' He tore his eyes away. 'What about it?'

156

She released her dress. It slipped down over her haunches to her knees. She smoothed it with her hands. 'Read the note Dane gave you,' she said.

He opened it curiously, looked at her, looked back at the note, swallowed hard and read aloud: 'There is a small, crescent-shaped scar high up in the hollow of the groin.'

'I hope that satisfies you, Inspector,' she said. 'Even a striptease party wouldn't show that much. Dane spent last night with me. That's how he knew.'

He swallowed. 'I guess that's kinda conclusive,' he said. He looked at Dane curiously. 'You got around to knowing this dame pretty quickly.'

Fuller got up from his chair slowly. His face was white and his eyes were hard with an inner hurt. 'I don't think you'll be needing me anymore,' he said. He was having trouble in keeping control of his voice.

'I guess not,' said Sharp. He shot a quick look at Pearl. 'I guess I'm sorry about this,' he added.

'Not at all, not at all,' said Leslie. He looked at Dane. 'You've given me quite an education,' he said.

'I feel bad about this,' said Dane awkwardly. 'I ...'

Leslie ignored him. He turned to Pearl. 'I wish you the best of luck,' he said. 'I'm sorry it had to be this way. I had hoped ...' There was a break in his voice. For a moment he tried to master it, and then he gave up. He turned around quickly and walked out of the office in a hurry. I guess no guy likes folk to see him when he starts to cry.

Pearl's eyes were pained. 'I've hurt him terribly,' she said.

'I was a swine,' said Dane. 'I shouldn't have come to you. Not even ...'

'It was my fault, Dane,' she said softly. 'I wanted

you to.'

'Jeepers!' mouthed Sharp. 'Get out of here, will ya? I've got work to do. And stick around. Maybe I'll want you again.'

Pearl and Dane were absorbed in each other. They were talking together, looking into each other's eyes. They drifted over towards the door. They seemed to have forgotten about me and Sharp.

'And don't leave those lying around my office!' roared Sharp.

I shook Pearl by the shoulder and pointed. She gave a little gasp, ran back to the front of Sharp's desk and bent down. She slipped the panties over her ankles, worked them up her calves, over her knees and up under her skirt. She reached the point where she'd have to lift her skirt to hoist them into position. She hesitated, looked at Sharp.

'Hurry up!' he roared.

'D'ya mind?' she asked.

'Hmph,' he snorted in consent. He held his head to one side and watched her keenly from the corner of his eyes. She hoisted quickly, there was a gleam of silken thighs and then she was buttoning.

'Kinda cute rig-out you young ladies wear these days,' said Sharp.

'You shouldn't be looking,' she said reprovingly.

'Well, of all the …!' he began.

She smoothed her skirt with her hands. It followed faithfully the curves of her body. 'I'm sorry if I've shocked you, Inspector,' she said.

'Well, of all the …!' he said again.

But she was back with Dane, taking his arm, following him out through the door.

I said awkwardly: 'Got any leads on this yet,

Sharp?'

He eyed me suspiciously. 'What are you getting at, Janson?'

I shrugged. 'Seems like you've been checking everyone – Skinner, Mrs Burden, Pearl Gibbons. I thought maybe you might even suspect me, or – or – Dane Morris or even Leslie Fuller.'

His eyes probed into me. 'You ain't trying to wheedle information outta me, are you, Janson?'

'Of course not,' I said. 'You've seen the *Chronicle*. We know who the murderer is.'

'Yeah,' he said. A dark flush spread over his face. 'Yeah, you're gonna show the cops, aren't you? Well, get out of here before I pinch you! I'm fed up with seeing you around. Clear off!'

I grinned, walked out slowly. I closed the door behind me, waited a few seconds, opened it quickly. Sharp was yelling into the telephone. He was saying: 'Check on that guy Fuller! Find out everything you can about him!'

I closed the door quietly. It seemed like I still had a good chance of beating Sharp to it.

I found Dane and Pearl arm in arm at the entrance to the station. They were waiting for a taxi. I came up behind them, said quietly in Dane's ear:

'Why did you do it, Dane?'

He turned in surprise. 'What are you talking about?'

'She'll have to know sometime,' I said. 'Might as well come clean. You killed him, didn't you? Why not admit it? It'll save a lotta trouble.'

He stared at me with wide eyes. 'Hank,' he said, 'you're crazy! You're stark, raving mad!'

11

We went into a nearby café, ordered coffee. I looked across the table at Pearl and shook my head wonderingly. 'Don't know how you two did it,' I said.

'Did what?'

'Just about 12 hours,' I said. 'The next thing, you're closer than man and wife!'

Her eyes were shining. 'It was just something that happened,' she said. 'It happened' – she snapped her fingers – 'just like that.'

'I can imagine,' I said drily. I snapped my fingers. 'Just like that!'

Dane was stirring his coffee thoughtfully. 'These things do happen,' he said quietly.

'You're a fast worker, lady,' I complimented her. 'I figure it pays off dividends, though.'

Dane gave me a hard look. 'You're not very bright,' he said. 'When Leslie Fuller walked out on Pearl back there just now, it was a million-buck husband walking out of the door.'

'Money ain't everything,' I said meaningfully.

Pearl looked at me with curious eyes. 'You think I've an ulterior motive?' she accused.

'Haven't you?' I leered.

She looked angry. 'I liked Dane the minute I saw him,' she said hotly. 'Just meeting somebody like that can change your feelings almost immediately.'

'I can think of other reasons,' I said.

'Such as?' Dane's voice was ugly. He wasn't liking me very much.

'The question is,' I said slowly, 'which of you two killed Burden?'

Dane said thoughtfully: 'I think I ought to sock you now.'

'Wait a minute,' said Pearl quickly. She looked at me earnestly. 'You must have a reason for saying that.'

'Sure,' I said. 'Wanna hear?'

'Yeah,' said Dane. 'Let's hear. If it's not good, I can take up the matter of that poke on the nose.'

'Dane's got plenty of motive for killing Burden,' I said. I looked meaningfully at Pearl.

She flushed. 'Dane's told me all about it,' she said. 'I can understand how he must have felt about Stella.'

'Yeah,' I said bitterly. 'He musta felt just the same way that guy Leslie Fuller must have felt.'

She had the grace to flush. 'It was better to break it to him quickly. It was honest.'

'Honest, maybe,' I said. 'But it didn't make it any more pleasant.'

'Stick to the point,' said Dane. 'I had plenty of motive for killing Burden. What's more, I asked for a gun last night. What's more, I had in mind killing him right then. Where does that get you?'

'Where it got you,' I said. 'Outside Burden's house a few minutes before he was killed.'

'I was there, too,' she said. 'I was waiting around the corner for Dane in the car.'

I stared at her. 'You went there with him?'

Dane said quietly: 'Wanna know what happened?'

I leaned back in my chair, lit a cigarette. I could anticipate the ground being knocked out from underneath my feet again.

'I went out again almost as soon as you dropped me last night,' said Dane. 'I was feeling sick about Stella. I was feeling so sick I wanted somebody to confide in. Pearl had given me her address. Late though it was, I went to see her. I just had to have somebody to confide in and company of some kind. Well, like Pearl's told you, there was just something between us. And something happened. We couldn't help it, neither of us.'

'It was my fault as much as his,' Pearl put in.

Dane went on: 'I don't quite know why it was. I guess I thought I was still in love with Stella. But I began wondering about her again. I was fretting, feeling sick inside. And Pearl could see it. And when finally I said I couldn't stand it any longer and was going to find out what had happened to her, Pearl said she'd drive me there. She's just that kinda girl. Understanding!'

Pearl wasn't looking at us, she had her head bowed and was tracing patterns on the table with her fingernail.

'I don't know quite what I intended to do,' said Dane. 'I was all steamed up. I guess I really wanted to find out what had happened to Stella, wanted to make sure that it was really that way. I guess maybe I wanted to see Burden, too. Have it out with him once and for all.

'But when I got there, I was all mixed up inside. Just seeing the place again made me feel even more sick. I wandered around the back of the house abstractedly, hardly knowing what I was doing. Then I called up to Stella's window, shouting her name and wondering whether Burden's head would poke out. But I only called a coupla times, and not very loudly at that. I didn't seem to have the heart to do it.

'Then I went around the front of the house and rang the bell. I rang only once. A short, sharp ring. I didn't get any reply. And then, quite suddenly, everything seemed different. I wondered what I was doing there. I wondered why I was bothering about Stella. Somehow, Stella didn't seem to matter anymore to me. I was remembering Pearl, the way she had been kind and understanding. And then I suddenly understood it was Pearl I really wanted deep down inside me. So I just left it at that. Left the house and went back to Pearl. She drove me back to her flat. I had breakfast with her and then went on to the *Chronicle* office. That's all that happened.'

'Is that on the level, Dane?' I asked.

'On the level,' he said. His eyes were staring straight into mine.

'Burden must have been murdered while you were outside the house, or almost immediately afterwards,' I mused.

'Why couldn't he have been murdered before I got there?' said Dane. 'I didn't get any reply to the front door. If he'd been downstairs in the lounge he'd have opened up, wouldn't he?'

It was on the tip of my tongue to say that the little man Carter had left Burden alive just a few moments earlier, and then I bit back. I wasn't giving away all my aces.

'You still could have done it, Dane,' I said.

'Maybe,' he said. 'I could have done it. If it hadn't been for Pearl, maybe I would have done it. But I didn't.'

'You were pretty jumpy this morning,' I said. 'Miserable, nervous, upset.'

He looked at me levelly. 'I wonder how you'd feel if you'd just lost your girl to Burden, then found the sweetest girl in the world, only to know she was about to marry a millionaire's son? Would you look happy?'

'No, I guess not,' I said abstractedly. Something he'd said was milling around in my mind. I got a vague hunch. I said suddenly: 'Excuse me a minute, will you?'

I went across to the telephone kiosk, fingered nickels into the slot. If you know how, it's possible to get a line through to any exchange switchboard as though you're a subscriber. I knew how to do it.

The dame said, 'Switchboard.'

'I wanna make some enquiries,' I said. I gave her a telephone number. 'I wanna check any calls that have gone out from here today.'

She was a smart operator. She said promptly: 'You made the calls. You should know.'

'Listen,' I said patiently, 'I'm the subscriber. I just pay the telephone bills. But I wanna check up on the people that's been using my phone. How about it?'

'Just a minute,' she said. She clicked off to attend to another call. Then clicked back again. 'What were you saying?'

'You've got a nice voice, honey,' I said, 'What do you do evenings?' I wanted information from that dame and was gonna get in good with her if possible.

'Cut that out, Romeo,' she said. 'I'm married. I got that way through taking up a blind date. You leave me cold.'

'Maybe you are married,' I said soothingly. 'But if your figure's like your voice, it must be a honey!'

'I measure 38, 32 and 38,' she said coldly. 'I've got varicose veins, my hair's almost grey and I've got two kids, one five and one seven. Now, will you stop trying to woo me?'

'They must be nice kids,' I said. 'I'd like to make them a present.'

'I've got those numbers,' she said coldly. 'Here they are.'

She started to give them to me and somebody else came on the line. 'Just a minute,' she said, and clicked off.

A moment later she clicked back again. Her voice was charged with suspicion. 'What's your game?' she demanded.

'I've told you.'

'That number you gave me's a phoney. I've just got a call come through from that number on another line.'

I took a deep breath. 'Okay, Goldilocks,' I said. 'I'll give it to you straight. I'm a private eye, see? I want some information.' Then I got inspiration. 'Listen,' I said eagerly. 'Put the guy through to this number. Let me listen in on it, will ya? You can fix it.'

'You know I can't do that,' she said. 'It's as much as my job's worth.'

'I'd like to make a present to your two kids,' I said. 'Mutual aid.'

'It's against the regulations,' she said crisply. 'Just a minute.' She clicked off.

I hung on a few moments and the wire clicked again. But this time I heard voices speaking. I held my breath and listened. I listened right through to the conversation's end. When it was over the operator clicked back on the line again.

'Are you still there?'

'Yes.'

'Now what do you want?'

'I guess it was an accident,' I said. 'Coupla lines got

crossed. I overheard other folk.'

'Is that so?' she said. 'Accidents do happen sometimes.' She sighed.

'What's your address?' I said. 'What do you call the kids?'

'You were on the level about that?'

'Mutual aid!'

'Much obliged, mister,' she said. "They can do with a present. Father's been laid up sick for the past four months.'

She gave me the address. I took careful note of it and went back to the table.

'Where are you two planning to go?' I asked.

Pearl looked at Dane and her eyes were bright. Happy, sparkling eyes. 'We've got plans,' she said.

'That's right,' said Dane. 'I won't be around for a few days. We're gonna take a trip to Las Vegas.'

'Las Vegas! That costs dough,' I said,

'I've saved a little,' said Pearl softly. 'Enough to get us there and a honeymoon.'

'Right in the middle of all this trouble!' I shook my head dismally.

'It's your worry,' said Dane. 'You started it. You finish it. I'm only the drama critic. Murder doesn't bother me unless it's on the stage.'

I looked at Pearl and I looked at Dane. 'You two really are nuts about each other, aren't you?'

He took her hand and squeezed it gently. 'We sure are!' he said. 'And what's your next move? Not that we wanna help. Just outta interest.'

'Yeah,' I said. 'I got things to do. I'd better get busy on them right now.'

'I'd like to give you plenty to think about,' said Dane. His eyes twinkled. 'Just so that criminal mind of yours gets plenty of exercise. Have you ever figured out there's a law in this country that excuses husband or wife from giving incriminating evidence against the other?'

I looked from one to the other of them suspiciously. I shook my head sadly. 'I still don't know,' I said. 'Maybe you killed him, maybe you didn't. But I'm going to give you the benefit of the doubt. I'm working on the angle you didn't do it, Dane.'

'In that case,' smiled Pearl, 'I'll wish you success.'

She was in a private ward. I eased open the door gently and looked across at her. She was a young dame, maybe 20. She was sleeping. She had long black hair that rippled over the pillow and against which her pale face seemed even whiter. There was a nurse sitting beside her, and as I opened the door she looked up and put one finger to her lips.

I backed out again, closed the door behind me and then turned to my doctor friend who'd used his influence in the hospital to let me see her.

'Can you tell me something about it?' I asked.

'I'm not supposed to, Hank,' he said.

'It won't go no further,' I assured him. 'Just between you and me.'

He shook his head sadly. 'Bad case,' he said. 'For a long time it was touch and go. We had to use the stomach pump. She's a strong girl, though. She made it. But she lost the baby.'

'Baby?'

He looked down at the floor. 'Yes, I guess that's why she did it. She's not married.' 'Police know about it? Will she be charged?'

'My job is to help people who are ill, Hank,' he said. 'If the police ask questions we give them information. But we don't have to do police work for them. Nobody's asked us if it is attempted suicide so we don't say anything. If she'd died it would have been different.'

'She's all right now, then?

'She'll make out,' he said. 'She's strong.'

'Now about this guy Williams,' I said. 'You say he was here all last evening with her?'

'Couldn't get rid of him,' he said. 'Just hung around. When she recovered consciousness he pleaded with us to see her. He was with her a little while and then dashed out.'

'What time would that be?'

'Early hours of the morning.'

'Have you seen him since?'

'I haven't seen him. But he's been ringing through regularly. The guy must be stuck on her. Might even have been the father of the child. He didn't look the type, though.'

'You've been helpful,' I said. 'Just one more thing. Could you let me have her address?'

'Well,' he doubted. 'It's very irregular.'

'So's all of this, including suicide,' I said. 'Just let me have the address. That's all I want.'

It was a gloomy residential district near Sleepy Hollow, boarding-house land. A third of the houses in the street exhibited rooms-to-let boards.

I left the taxi waiting outside the door of the house, found the name I was looking for on the indicator board and climbed steadily and heavenwards up dusty, gloomy stairs to the fifth floor.

There were three apartments on that floor. I picked the one I wanted, rapped hard on panels from which old paint was peeling.

'Who is it?' a dame asked.

'Open up!' I said loudly. 'Open up!' I rapped more vigorously on the panels.

She opened up quickly. She was only a kid and her eyes were frightened.

'Wanna talk with you,' I said. 'Police.'

She opened up like I'd come to arrest her for murder and she was too scared to resist arrest. She'd pulled a red dressing-gown around her and I could see it was covering underclothing.

I shot a quick glance around. It was the kinda apartment you'd expect a coupla dames of 20 or so to occupy. A coupla single beds, badly made, and the rest of the room a riot of disorder. Cheap, old-fashioned furniture supplied by the landlady. Clothes, hanging behind the door, draped across chairs, hanging out of half-closed drawers. A dressing-table littered with toilet preparations, stockings on the mantelpiece, hairbrushes, combs, soap and boxes of bath cubes on the table, together with an open butter-dish, half-cut loaf and a pile of dirty crockery.

She worked up a weak smile. 'I'm afraid – I wasn't expecting – it's a little untidy.'

'I haven't come to see the place,' I told her. 'Just to ask a few questions.'

'Won't you sit down?' she said. She was nervous as a cat. Her hands were fluttery.

I removed a slipper from a chair, shifted some dirty underclothing and settled down. Meanwhile, the dame hurriedly and clumsily took down the smalls hanging on a line stretched across the room. She thrust them away hurriedly beneath the table.

I tried to look like a cop. I tried to talk like a cop. 'You're Jane Symons,' I said.

She bit her lip. 'That's right, sir.'

'You live here with Rita Clark.'

She hung her head. 'That's right, sir,' she admitted. Her voice was almost a whisper.

'Yesterday evening she was taken to hospital, very ill. You telephoned for the ambulance. Is that right?'

'That's right,' she said. She was still hanging her head and I hardly heard her this time.

'Are you aware of the nature of her illness?'

'Yes,' she said, and this time I didn't hear her.

'Speak up.'

'Yes,' she said, more loudly.

'You know she attempted suicide?'

'Yes,' she admitted. You'd have thought she was a convicted prisoner, humbled and ashamed of herself and confessing to terrible crimes.

'Don't be so worried,' I said gently. 'You haven't done anything to be ashamed of. I just want you to answer the questions, that's all. You did your duty. You had her taken to hospital.'

'I didn't know she was going to do it,' she said suddenly. 'I would have stopped her. But I didn't know.'

'Of course not,' I said gently. 'Do you know why she may have done this?'

She nodded again. 'She was …'

I looked down myself. 'I'm afraid she won't have it now,' I said.

After a long pause she said: 'I'm sorry.'

'Well, now' I said. 'Let's see what else we can find out.'

She was a good talker. She just answered yes or no to questions, but when talking gave every scrap of information she knew.

Rita Clark and she were both employed as hat-check girls at the Storkers Club. They started work at eight in the evening and carried on until four or five in the morning. The previous evening at about six o'clock, Jane had come in from shopping to find Rita writhing on the bed, her face contorted in agony and a bottle of poison lying at her side. Jane had been a sensible girl. She'd telephoned the hospital immediately.

She'd gone to the hospital in the ambulance, she'd waited as long as she could and then gone on to her job. By that time she'd learned there was a 50-50 chance that Rita would live.

'This is important,' I said. 'Do you know who the father of the child was?'

She nodded dumbly.

'You'll have to tell me,' I said. 'Who was it?'

She almost choked over the words. 'Hugh Burden,' she said.

The hunch I'd been working on wasn't a hunch any longer. Suddenly I knew this was it. This was the real break. Now I was really getting somewhere.

I asked more questions. It seemed Hugh Burden had been a frequenter at the Storkers Club. He was the type of guy to be taken by a pretty face. All was grist that came to Burden's love mill. Even a hat-check girl. So he'd worked on her innocence and her youth. The affair had been only fleeting, Burden dropping Rita almost as soon as he'd used her.

She'd kept the secret as long as she could, until her room-mate, young but wise in the ways of the world, had three-quarters guessed the truth. It had all been pent up inside Rita, too much for her to bear alone. She'd confided in Jane, told her everything, and Jane had sympathised. Not that it helped any. The one person who could help was Hugh Burden. And he'd just laughed at her, accused her of trying to blackmail him.

'Rita's a good girl,' said Jane. 'He was the only one. There was never anybody else. She thought the world of him, too. Even though he'd deserted her that way.'

I was getting the picture clearly now. I said: 'What do you know about a guy named Williams?'

She took the question in her stride. 'A nice little guy,' she said. 'Used to come into the club two or three times a week and talk with Rita.' Then she looked at me angrily. 'You're not suggesting –'

I held up my hand. 'I'm not suggesting anything. I'm just asking questions.'

'There was nothing to it,' she said hotly. 'He was a nice old guy. More like a father.'

The word 'father' clicked in my mind.

'Did Rita ever tell you his exact relationship to her?'

'He wasn't any relation,' she said. 'He was just a friend. He used to call in two or three times a week. He only came to speak to Rita. He was interested in her.'

'Did Rita ever tell you why he was interested in her?'

'To be honest,' she said, 'it seemed a bit funny to me. Rita was studying in her spare time. He used to give her money to help her. We don't get good wages at the club. He used to buy her books and give her money for clothes. I believe he paid her school fees, too.'

'And all that for nothing!'

'It wasn't like that. Honest. When he first started it, Rita tried to discourage him. Then, as it went on, it was clear he didn't expect anything. I guess he was one of those guys who'd got a lotta dough and just liked doing things for people.' She pouted. 'He never offered to help me.'

'Just one more thing,' I said. 'Do you know where Rita Clark was born?'

'That's easy,' she said. 'We used to go up to school together. That's why we got this job together. North River Side.'

'Thanks very much, Jane,' I said. 'You've been very helpful. Very helpful indeed.'

There were tears glimmering in her eyes. 'Is she going to be all right – I mean – Rita?'

'She's going to be all right,' I reassured her. 'Just as soon as she's better she'll come home.'

'Won't you …?' She looked upon me as a cop.

'We'll forget all about it,' I said. 'When a kid's had a tough time, we don't wanna make it worse.' I went across to the door and noticed the butter and the cut loaf on the table. I thought how tough it was for two young dames to make a living and pay their expenses in Chicago. I thought how difficult it was going to be for Jane, paying for that apartment from her slender wage-packet while Rita was still in hospital. She had a pale, hungry look like she didn't get enough to eat.

'Look, kid,' I said. 'You're going to look after Rita, aren't you?'

'Of course,' she said. 'Rita's my best friend.'

I took out my wallet, peeled off five century notes. 'Put this towards the rent,' I said. 'It's gonna be a few weeks before she gets back to work.'

She stared at the money with eager eyes. Then she looked at me sadly.

'No thanks, mister,' she said. 'I couldn't take it,

honest. It's awfully good of you, but I could never pay it back.'

'Take it, kid. You don't have to pay it back,' I growled.

'I couldn't take it,' she gulped. 'But, if you wouldn't mind, mister. If you could give me just five bucks. Just so as I could buy some flowers for Rita.'

I reached out for her hand, pressed her fingers around the notes. 'Don't be a dope, kid,' I said. 'You can't fight the world alone.'

There were tears of gratitude in her eyes. She was trying to say something, thank me, but her lips were quivering with emotion. I turned away quickly, went out and closed the door behind me.

Chicago was a big town. If you wanted to be a writer you didn't have to dig deep to find material. All over town at that very minute there were a million homes where every degree of tragedy and happiness was being enacted. You only had to scratch the surface a little to find grim reality.

I'd just scratched the surface. Not very much, just a little. But as I went down those dark, gloomy stairs, I was blinking my eyes and telling myself not to be a big sentimental dope.

12

I arrived at the registrar's office just before it closed. I used my Press card, a lot of persuasion and dollars to get a coupla clerks working overtime. It was all adding up. I got the information I expected to get and it still added up. It all made sense now.

But I still had to swing it, and swinging it was going to be a problem. Hugh Burden's murderer was a guy who sounded like he was gonna stay quiet. I had to figure out some way to make him come out in the open.

The newspaper stands were crowded. Headlines were shrieking the news that the police were looking for Hugh Burden's missing secretary. That caused a flutter of anxiety in my belly.

I fought to buy a copy of the *Chronicle*. It was still pumping out the challenge. It couldn't do anything else. It was sink or swim now.

And the paradox was that the *Chronicle* had published on the front page a photograph of Carter, asking for information of his whereabouts, emphasising that Carter was wanted by the police for interviewing. And we had to publish that, knowing full well that when Carter told his story to Sharp it would alibi Skinner, proving that Skinner couldn't possibly have committed the murder.

I wondered what line Sharp was working on now. I gave it a try-out. I rang through to Police Headquarters. Sharp and Conrad were both out. I asked to be put through to someone in their office.

A dame answered the phone. Her voice sounded like she was 16. It seemed everybody else was out of the office. I asked: 'Do you know where Inspector Sharp is now?'

'He's interviewing witnesses,' she said. She had a vague, childlike voice.

'You know who?'

'I can find out,' she said eagerly. She came back to the phone, read out a list of the witnesses Sharp had interviewed. He'd have brained her if he'd known she was doing that!

'And where is he right now?'

She told me. Right then, it seemed, Sharp was at Lulu's apartment, testing her out for an alibi.

I chuckled to myself as I hung up. Lulu was a man-killer and Sharp was a prude. Interviewing her was a job that would scare the pants off him. She'd construe his every second question as an invitation to go to bed. I guessed he'd be sweating, and plenty!

I drove the car out to the Chief's cabin. It was quiet there, with an uninhabited look. I knocked at the door, waited. I knocked again. Still no reply. That pleased me. Carter was following our instructions. I opened up with the key the Chief had given me, and Carter met me in the lobby, his face worried and his eyes anxious.

'Oh, it's you,' he said, relieved.

'Sure,' I said. 'I wanna talk with you.'

'I want to see you, Mr Janson. I think I ought to go

to the police.'

'Cut that out,' I said tersely. 'I wanna talk.'

'But I want to tell you,' he said. 'I think I ought to go to the police station and tell them ...'

'Shuddup!' I gritted. I seized him by the shoulders, twisted him around and steered him back into the living-room. I thrust him down in a chair and said: 'Hold it. Shut up. We've gotta talk.'

I hung my hat on the arm of a chair, sat at the table opposite him and pulled a sheaf of certificates from my pocket.

'I'm gonna tell you a story, Carter,' I said. 'I'm gonna tell it briefly and to the point. I want you to listen to me. I don't want a word from you throughout the whole time I'm speaking. Understand?'

He nodded, his eyes wide.

'Not a word. Understand?'

He nodded again.

I leaned back in the chair and looked at the ceiling.

'Once upon a time,' I said, 'there was a guy who got married. That wasn't so unusual. They had a kid, too. That wasn't unusual, either. He had the kid the first year he was married, and deserted his wife the second year. That *was* unusual. He deserted his wife and kid, leaving them penniless.'

Carter's eyes were wide.

I fumbled through the certificates. I fished out one and put it down on the table in front of him. 'Copy of his marriage certificate,' I said. I added another to it. 'Birth certificate.' Then I riffled through and found another. I put that on top of the others. 'That's a divorce certificate,' I said. 'You see, the wife got herself another husband. His name was Clark. And being sensible folks and conscious of public prejudice, they changed the name of the little girl, too, so that she became Rita Clark.' I added another certificate to the little pile in front of him.

Carter looked at them. His eyes were wide, staring at me.

'Time passed,' I went on. 'Rita grew to be 17, attending college, her parents humble but careful. Then, three years ago, the worst happened. Mother and father were both killed in a car accident.'

I paused and Carter opened his mouth like he was gonna say something. 'Hold it,' I said. 'You can talk later.'

I went on. 'She was only a kid but she did her best. She got a job and tried to keep up her studies in her spare time. But things were tough. She drifted from job to job and finally got the position of hat-check girl at the Storkers Club. She wasn't earning a fortune either. Just a bare existence.'

Again he opened his mouth like he was going to say something. 'Shuddup, for heaven's sake,' I growled. 'Let me finish, will ya?'

His mouth closed like a trap. He was about the most obedient guy I've ever met.

'Well, round about a coupla years ago,' I went on, 'the girl's real father got a pang of conscience. He began to check up on his daughter He found out what had happened to her. And that was when his conscience finally began to hurt. You see, either Rita Clark had been brought up to believe her mother's second husband was her real father, or alternatively that her first father had deserted her mother. In the first place, she didn't know she had a real father alive, and in the second place if she did know, she'd know he was a skunk.'

I continued: 'So the guy couldn't let her know his real relationship to her. But he tried to make up to her for the trouble he had caused. He struck up an acquaintance with her and, having broken down her reserve, helped her in little ways where he could, paying for her schooling, making her presents of clothing, helping her in many little ways.'

I took out a cigarette, lit it, blew smoke towards the ceiling. 'I kinda like him for that,' I said. 'Maybe he behaved badly in the beginning, but everybody makes mistakes. He was trying to make up for it.'

Carter half rose out of his chair with his mouth open, wanting to say something. I waved him back again.

'Some months ago,' I continued, 'Rita Clark met Hugh Burden. He treated her like he treated all women. She was just the plaything of the moment. But she was innocent and she was young. She didn't understand these things. She thought she was in love and when he ditched her there were unfortunate complications, She bottled it all up inside her – despair, futility, frustration and hopelessness – and to a girl of her age it seemed a much more terrible thing than it was. Finally, yesterday evening about six o'clock, her room-mate came home from shopping and found her writhing on the bed with a bottle of poison at her side.'

Carter was still staring at me, but now his eyes had hardened just sufficiently for it to be noticeable.

'Her room-mate had sense,' I said. 'She called for an ambulance. She herself went with Rita to the hospital. They operated there. She lost the baby but her life was saved. Her room-mate, Jane, went on to the Storkers Club, and that night the girl's father, who was known all this time as Williams, called to see Rita and found out what had happened. Not all the story, just enough to make him anxious.

'He rushed over to the hospital and paced the wards for hours. Just the kinda thing a real father would do. He stopped there until they assured him she was out of danger and let him see her just for a little while.

'Williams knew his daughter had tried to commit suicide. He'd also learned why. There was just one thing he wanted to know. The name of the man who had caused it. And I guess in those few minutes while he was with his daughter she whispered the name Hugh Burden to him.'

Carter leaned forward in his chair now, listening intently.

'He felt the way most fathers would have felt. Moreover he knew just the kinda guy Burden was. There was only one thought in his mind then. Revenge!'

I waited a moment to let the effect of my words sink in. Then I went on quietly: 'He went over to Burden's house, found Burden, slipped a knife into his ribs.'

I got up, walked over to the window and stood looking out with my back towards Carter. 'I can't say I blame him for doing it,' I said. 'But, just the same, it was murder. The police are looking for the murderer now.' Then I turned around and looked at him steadily. 'I've got most of the facts,' I said. I pointed to the pile of certificates on the table. 'They build up a pretty clear picture. The police don't know who the murderer is. I do know who he is.' I looked at him levelly. 'The trouble is, I can't prove who he is – yet.'

His eyes were big like saucers.

'I've followed this hunch all the way through,' I went on. 'It finally comes down to just one thing. Either Dane Morris was lying when he said he couldn't get a reply when he rang the bell at Burden's house this morning, or' – I took a deep breath – 'or you were lying when you said Burden was alive at the time Dane came around the house.'

He said quietly: 'May I speak now?'

'Just a minute,' I said. 'I just wanna make this clear, Carter. You thought you might get suspicion switched to Dane Morris by saying you saw him at Burden's house this morning. But you'll have to make that stand up in court. And there's a dozen ways you may have slipped up. You musta taken a taxi from the hospital to Burden's house. The taxi-driver will remember. You thought it was clever to answer the *Chronicle*'s reward offer for information leading to the arrest of the murderer. But every link in the chain of your defence will have to be tested.' I indicated the pile of certificates. 'All that will be produced in court. All that will stand against you.'

'May I speak now?' he said quietly.

'I'm not going to let you get away with it, Carter,' I said. 'I'm gonna keep you here. If necessary, I'll chain you down. I'll keep you here until I find some way to prove you murdered Burden.'

'May I speak now?'

'Yeah,' I breathed. 'But it won't do you any good. I'll get you in the end.'

His wide eyes were fixed on mine. He said quietly: 'I've been trying to tell you, Mr Janson. You wouldn't let me tell you when you first came. I want to go down to the police station. I want to confess that I murdered Hugh Burden.'

I gaped at him. 'You want to confess?'

He nodded. 'I didn't know what I was doing this morning. After I'd killed Burden I wanted to run away, yet I wanted to be near Rita. I couldn't bear not to be near her and know what was happening. So then I thought I'd try to involve somebody else. Anything so I could remain free and keep in touch with Rita. That's why I came to your office and told you about Dane Morris.'

I breathed a sigh of relief. 'That's lets out Morris, anyway.'

'It was a wicked thing for me to do,' he went on quietly. He put his hand to his head as though it ached. 'I think I was out of my mind at the time. I would never have let them do anything to him.' He screwed up his forehead as though he was suffering from some pain. 'I'm not afraid to pay for what I did. It's just that – I was out of my mind.'

'You don't have to feel so bad about it,' I said. 'Hugh Burden's got a bad reputation. When you tell the court the facts, tell them about Rita and what happened to her, you'll get clemency.'

'No,' he said anxiously. 'They mustn't know that. They mustn't know anything about that.'

I stared at him. 'Are you crazy?'

'Don't you see?' he pleaded, and there were tears in his eyes. 'I've already harmed Rita too much. She doesn't know about me. She knows me only as Williams. And if it all comes out – she'll know then that her father is a murderer, too!'

It kinda stunned me for a moment, seeing it in that light. I said: 'Well, what are you going to do? You've gotta look after yourself. You've gotta enter a plea of some kind.'

'No, Mr Janson,' he said quietly. 'I've been thinking it over all the time I've been here. I'm going to admit I killed Hugh Burden. I'm going to say I had no reason. I worked for him and I disliked him, and in a moment of temper I killed him.'

'You won't be able to go through with it,' I told him. 'You might have the best intentions now. It's when you're in court, when you know you're on trial for your life, when you realise that the chair is the ultimate end, that you'll wanna fight. Everybody fights to live. It's the law of life.'

He shook his head sadly. 'It's different for me, Mr Janson,' he said. He touched his chest just about where his heart would be. 'I've been under the doctors for a long time. They gave me three years to live, four years ago. My heart's very bad. I'm liable to drop dead any time.' He worked up a weak smile. 'I've thought about dying quite a lot,' he said seriously. 'You get a feeling, you know. You know it's gonna be all right. You know what the doctors say isn't really so serious. And then later you get another kinda feeling. You know that, after all, the doctors were right. You've got a feeling inside you that tells you –' He paused, licked his lips, and added: 'You don't have to worry about me, Mr Janson. The law can inflict no penalty that worries me.'

He added quietly: 'If I ever pay the penalty.'

After he'd finished talking, I stood for a long moment thinking in silence. I felt a new respect for this man. I felt mean about the role I was playing. But one has to be a realist. One has to face facts.

'Would you like to tell me how it happened? For the paper, I mean.'

'It was very simple,' he said. 'As you remember, during the party I had a headache. I went out for a walk to clear my head. I went for a long walk through Central Park. I walked all the time and then came back during the early morning.' He looked at me meaningfully. 'You understand that perfectly, don't you?'

I understood well enough. He was covering up the

185

fact that he had been at the hospital waiting for news of Rita Clark.

'And this is what really happened,' he said. 'I let myself into the house. It was about half-past six. The place was a shambles as you know. But the door of the little room next to the kitchen was open and I could hear Burden snoring. Up until then I hadn't any definite plans. I just knew I wanted to kill him. I wondered what I should use for a weapon, and remembered the paper-knife in the study.

'Burden was lying on the settee, fast asleep. He wasn't even wearing a shirt. I crept up to him, knelt down beside him and poised the paperknife carefully. I could see the outline of his ribs and it was easy to aim between them. I did it quickly, darting forward, pressing down my whole weight. I was surprised how easily it went in. He gave a loud cry and his arms waved like he was trying to fight off somebody. Still the knife still hadn't gone all the way in and I thrust harder. It needed all my strength to make it go in up to the hilt. And it kinda jammed between his ribs. Then one of his fists caught me and knocked me over.'

'He didn't die right away?'

'It was an awful thing,' he said in a hushed voice. 'If it had been anybody else I should have felt terrible about it. But it seemed so right for him, so right he should suffer himself after causing so much suffering to others.'

'Did he know it was you?'

Carter nodded. 'He kept on moaning. He musta been in dreadful pain. And when he saw it was me he pulled himself up off the settee. I could see he wanted to launch himself at me, smash me the same way as he used to punch other fellas. But he hadn't the strength. He stood there swaying, staring at me and pulling on the knife-handle trying to get it out. But he didn't try very hard, he hadn't the strength.'

'Were you wearing gloves?' I asked.

'I didn't use gloves,' he said. 'But there was a garment lying on the floor by the side of the settee. I think it's called a G-string. I wrapped that around the haft of the knife before I used it.'

I nodded. 'I've seen it,' I said.

Carter went on: 'I don't know where he got the strength, but he staggered across to me like he was going to attack. I backed away from him and he followed me out of the little room, along the passage and into the lounge. It was dreadful to see him that way. He musta been in agony. And yet somehow he was keeping himself on his feet. He followed me half-way across the lounge before his knees finally gave way beneath him. He lay on the floor, and all the time he was looking up at me accusingly. I stood there watching him. I don't know how long I musta stood there watching him. It may have been minutes, it may have been longer. And then quite suddenly I realised he wasn't alive any longer.

'I was just going out through the front door when I heard somebody coming up the path. It was Dane Morris. I didn't want him to see me. He did ring the bell, and finally he went away. I followed out almost immediately after him.'

'That's just how it happened?'

'Just that way.'

I said awkwardly: 'D'ya mind if I phone into my paper? They'd like to get the news first.'

'I'd like you to do that, Mr Janson,' he said. He smiled wryly. 'I understand that the prestige of your paper is at stake.'

I got through to the Chief, gave him the full story. He took it down, word for word, as I gave it to him. He said: 'Give me half an hour, will you, and I'll have it on the streets!'

'It'll take all of that for Sharp to get out here,' I said.

'Good enough,' he replied. 'I'll have every news-hawk in town at the police station waiting to see them when they come in.'

I turned around to Carter. 'Ready now?' I asked quietly.

He nodded. 'I'm ready anytime. We go now?'

'Better than that,' I said. 'We make them come here.'

I dialled the Homicide Department. I asked for Sharp. He'd just arrived in the office.

'Janson here,' I told him.

'What's biting you?' he demanded.

'I've got the murderer here. It'll look good if you come out and get him. It'll be better than if I bring him in.'

He almost burst. 'Where are you?' he demanded.

I gave him the address. He smashed down the receiver without saying goodbye. I guessed he'd be ordering out squad cars and plenty of cops like he was bringing in a homicidal maniac. It amused me he'd taken my word for it without even asking the identity of the murderer.

'You will help me, won't you?' said Carter. 'You understand my position. Rita must never know I'm her father.'

'There's only you and me know that,' I said. I gathered up all the copy certificates, put them in the fireplace and applied a match to them.

'I knew you were kind the first time I met you,' he said. He fumbled in his pocket and pulled out a cheque book. 'Would you do one other thing for me?'

'Anything that's possible.'

'I've saved a little money,' he said. 'Just over a thousand dollars. It's all I have in the world. I'd like Rita to have it. She mustn't know it's from me. If I make the cheque out to you, will you see she gets it? She'll need medical attention and something to help her with her studies.'

'I'll do better than that,' I said. 'I'll put another thousand dollars to it.' I mopped my brow. 'Letting me have your confession before you gave it to the police has saved the *Chronicle* a coupla hundred grand. Maybe they'll kick in something, too.'

'I hope so,' he said. He signed the cheque, handed it to me. I folded it away in my wallet and there was a choked feeling in my throat. I had to admire the lug. He was going to die. He knew it and he was unconcerned. He was thinking only about his daughter and trying to do something for her.

'I never smoke, Mr Janson,' he said. 'But just this one occasion, would you–?'

'Sure,' I said. I pulled out my cigarettes and offered him one. I took one myself and we both lit up.

He looked at me broodingly. 'You must be a very intelligent man, Mr Janson. How did you find out about my daughter?'

'When I telephoned you here,' I said, 'the line was engaged. Later, when I finally got through, you denied the line had been engaged. I didn't think anything of it then. But later I had to make a decision. I had to believe either that Dane Morris was lying or that you were lying. I began with an assumption. I assumed you were lying.

In that case you must have had a motive. And then I remembered your phone call.

'I tried to trace where that phone call was made to. I had luck. The telephone operator was helpful. She cross-lined me just at the time when you were speaking to the hospital. I heard you asking about Miss Clark.' I shrugged my shoulders. 'From then on it was easy. I went to the hospital, found out about Rita, learned more about the Mr Williams who'd been pacing the ward all night and who was also calling to see her two or three times a week where she worked. It was obviously you. I wondered why you should be so interested in Rita Clark. It was the room-mate who put me on to it. She said your attitude was that of a father. It was a lead. I followed it up at the registrar's office and it yielded results.'

'It's only when we get older we realise how wrong we were when young,' he mused. 'Things could have been so different if I hadn't …'

His voice tailed off.

'What happened to the woman you went away with?'

A cynical smile twisted his lips. 'She treated me as I deserved to be treated. She fooled me, spent every penny I had and finally went off with somebody else.' His clear eyes looked at me. 'You see, I've suffered, too.'

Not long afterwards, cars screeched to a standstill outside. The hammering on the door sounded like they were trying to break it down. I opened up and Sharp and Conrad and two or three uniformed cops charged in like they were raiding a bootlegging joint.

'Take it easy, fellas,' I said. 'Take it easy.'

'What the hell's all this about?' yelled Sharp.

I smiled easily. 'I want to introduce you to somebody,' I said. 'Mr Burden's secretary.' I nodded towards Carter, who was standing quietly in the doorway of the living-room. He was such a nondescript little man, Sharp almost missed seeing him.

'What the hell's he doing here?' yelled Sharp. Then his eyes lighted up. 'You've been concealing a material witness!'

'I haven't been concealing him,' I objected. 'Mr Carter wishes to make a confession.'

Sharp glared. His eyes switched around to Carter. 'What's he talking about?' he asked.

'It's perfectly true,' said Carter. He swallowed nervously. 'You see, I'm Hugh Burden's secretary. I killed him this morning.' He swallowed again. 'I just couldn't stand him any longer. He was driving me crazy. He was paying me poor wages and everything I did was wrong. I couldn't stand it any longer.'

The wind came out of Sharp like the air coming out of a pricked balloon. Then he flared round to face me. 'What are you doing here? What's it got to do with you?'

'If you'll allow me to explain,' said Carter quickly. 'I telephoned Mr Janson. I said I wished to speak to him. I wouldn't tell him where I was. I asked him to meet me somewhere. Mr Janson suggested this place, which I believe belongs to the Editor of the *Chronicle*. I met him here, made my confession and he telephoned you.'

'What goes on?' demanded Sharp angrily. 'Why in hell can't people come to the cops in the first place instead of going to news-hawks?'

'Perhaps,' suggested Carter with just a wisp of a smile around his lips. 'Perhaps they have more respect for reporters.'

Sharp said to one of the cops: 'Put the bracelets on him.'

He was such a nondescript little man. Yet they

moved in on him burlily and massively. Two of them. Each handcuffed themselves to Carter. He gave me a brave little smile as much as to say, '*As if I'd try to escape, anyway.*'

Then Sharp spun round to face me. 'You're not so smart, Janson,' he sneered. 'You think you're gonna get away to start telephoning. Well, you've made a mistake. You're coming down the station, too. You're gonna have a lot of talking to do. It's gonna be hours before you get back to your paper.' He jerked his thumb towards the door. 'Come on, get going!'

I smiled. 'You don't mind if I smoke?' I asked.

'Get going!' he growled.

We arrived at Police Headquarters in grand style. Two motorbikes went ahead, sirening through the traffic. I was in the front car with Sharp and Conrad, and Carter was brought along in the car behind.

It looked as though the whole of Chicago was gathered around the steps leading up to the station precinct when the cars slewed into the kerb and ground to a stop. We climbed out of the cars and immediately there were flashbulbs popping everywhere. Carter was using his head. He didn't want Rita to know he was her father. He got one of the cops to hold his cap in front of his face. Not that it mattered, anyway. Who ever saw a newspaper photograph that looked like the subject?

It made a nice picture – those two big cops going up the steps with that poor little man handcuffed between them. And the bulbs went on flashing all the way up the steps. I thought Sharp looked a little surprised, and I chuckled to myself.

Once inside we were hustled through to the

Homicide Department. I hung around while Carter was formally charged with murder and he insisted right away on writing out a confession. That satisfied everybody, because with a written confession, it was in the bag. It satisfied Sharp and it satisfied Carter.

And when Carter was taken away to the cells, Sharp turned to me.

'Now we'll deal with you,' he said and rubbed his hands.

'What exactly do you want?'

'Just between you and me,' he said nastily, 'I wanna keep you here just so long that you can't get a story out on the streets. And, just to make it official, I'm gonna keep you here for questioning, and ...' He broke off. Conrad was at his elbow, tugging him. He turned around. 'Don't bother me now,' he scowled.

'I think you ought to see this,' said Conrad. He pushed it under Sharp's nose.

I looked at it over Sharp's shoulder. It was the *Chronicle*. And in banner headlines across the page it boasted: '*Chronicle Cracks Burden Murder!*'

Underneath that, in smaller type, it said: '*Hank Janson*, Chronicle's *star reporter, has fulfilled the* Chronicle's *guarantee to find the murderer of Hugh Burden before the police were able to do so.*'

Sharp's cheeks were flaming. He could hardly speak. He rolled up the paper and stuttered: 'Where did this come from?'

'They were selling it outside 20 minutes before we arrived,' said Conrad. 'That's why all the newsboys were here. Every reporter in town knows the *Chronicle* had the news out before we brought him in.'

Sharp turned towards me, trembling with anger. 'You – you –!' he stammered.

'That's saved the *Chronicle* a coupla hundred grand,' I said. 'Reads nice, too, don't it?'

He almost exploded. He would have attacked me if the station hadn't been crawling with cops and reporters. He contented himself with ripping the newspaper into pieces.

I grinned at him cheekily. 'I take it I won't be required for questioning now?' I said gently.

'Get out!' roared Sharp. 'Get out!'

I drifted out down the station steps. There were still a lot of newsboys there. The flashbulbs went on flashing. Just to make the story good, I bought a copy of the *Chronicle* and posed with it in front of me while they took more pictures.

I supposed I should have felt pleased with life. But I wasn't. There were one or two things nagging at the back of my mind. This case wasn't wrapped up yet. I wasn't going to be happy until everything fitted together and made sense.

I went back to the office and into the Chief's room. I gave him the true story, exactly as it was. He was the kinda guy you could talk with that way.

And when I was through he said: 'You've missed out on a lot of things.'

'That's what worries me,' I said. 'I've gotta sort them out.'

I sat at the desk, wrote out some expenses chits. 'Okay these, will you?' I asked.

He looked at them. 'Five thousand bucks for Rita Clark. Two hundred bucks for Mrs Saunders!' He puckered his eyebrows.

'Rita Clark's father saved us two hundred grand,' I pointed out. 'Mrs Saunders helped. Her two kids could do with a present. Their father's sick.'

He initialled the chits. 'Tell the cashier to send them off,' he said.

I got as far as the door and he called: 'By the way, Hank. What did you do with that Lulu dame?'

'I ditched her,' I said. 'Lost her on the subway.'

'She keeps ringing me,' he complained. 'Wants to know if you're gonna keep your promise.'

'Jeepers!' I said.

He glared. 'Make sure you do keep that promise,' he said. 'I don't want that dame around my neck for the rest of my life.'

13

Skinner was at Dorothy's house when I arrived. They were having dinner together and I was invited to stay.

I excused myself. I had other things to do.

'There's one or two things I want to get straightened out, though,' I added.

Dorothy's eyes were slightly puzzled. 'Such as?'

'It's you, Charles,' I said. 'Why did you go back to Burden's house last night?'

'But I didn't,' he said. 'I didn't go there at all.'

'I'm sure Mr Janson understands,' said Dorothy smoothly. 'You see, it was quite natural. When I heard Hugh was killed I immediately thought that Charles might have been stupid enough to do it. I tried to give him an alibi. I said he was here last night.'

'I know he wasn't,' I said.

'You do?'

'I dropped in,' I said, 'just about the time you'd crossed over to get a sleeping draught. I knew Skinner hadn't been here.'

'And you said nothing?'

'Probably for the same reason *I* said nothing,' said Skinner. He looked at Dorothy tenderly. 'You see, when

Dorothy began to stress I was with her last night, I thought she wanted an alibi herself. So I accepted what she said, pretended I was here with her.'

'But you did go back to Burden's house,' I insisted.

'Not at all,' he said. 'I went out. I was so upset by what had happened I couldn't sleep. I went out and walked the streets. I arrived back just about seven o'clock. At no time was I within ten miles of Burden's house,'

'What about your fountain pen?' I said. 'You left it at Burden's house last night. This morning when I saw Burden lying there dead, the fountain pen wasn't on the mantelpiece. That means you must have come back sometime during the night and got it.'

He frowned. 'You're all mixed up,' he said. 'I did leave last night and leave my fountain pen. But I remembered it before I reached the road, returned for it.' He furrowed his brow, trying to remember. 'There was a young lady, Lulu I think she was called. As soon as she saw me, she rushed over to the mantelpiece and got my pen down for me.'

'I didn't see you,' I said.

'You weren't there at the time,' he said. 'I didn't notice you either.'

Then it hit me. 'Lulu actually saw you take that fountain pen?'

'Yes,' he said. 'Is that strange?'

'Very strange,' I said grimly. 'You'll have to excuse me, folks. I've got some visiting to do.'

A little later I was hammering at Lulu's door. It was an appreciable while before she got the door open, and when she did her face was flushed, her hair tumbled and she wore a dressing-gown tied loosely around her.

Her eyes lighted up when she saw me. 'Hank,' she said delightedly. 'I'm so pleased to see you. How stupid of me to lose you this morning. I've been so wanting to see you.'

'I wanna see you, too,' I said grimly.

And then she looked anxious. 'Hank,' she said. 'I'm gonna take a shower right now. Will you come back in ten minutes?'

'I'll wait,' I said.

'No,' she said urgently. 'You mustn't wait! Come back in ten minutes. I'll be ready for you then.'

She'd been standing in the doorway, holding the door half-closed. I put my hand against the door, shoved hard and pushed my way past her.

She shut the door, circled around in front of me, nervous and agitated. 'I do wish you'd come back later, Hank,' she pleaded.

I eased myself down in a chair, stared fixedly across the room at a fedora hanging on a hook, and said: 'I'll go soon. There's just one thing I wanna ask. When you tell me that, I'll go.'

'You'll come back?'

'That depends.' I said. I kept staring at the fedora. After a while she saw what I was looking at, raised a weak smile and said: 'That belongs to a friend of mine.'

'Looks like it might fit me.'

'Yes, it might,' she said. She looked uneasy.

'Let's have a look at it.'

She brought it over and I gave it the once-over, turned it over in my hands, looked at the hat-band. There were initials on the hat-band. That confirmed what I'd first thought. That hat had looked familiar to me.

'Want you to tell me something,' I said. 'Last night

at the party. Do you remember when Dorothy Burden and Charles Skinner went on home?'

She nodded.

'I went upstairs,' I said. 'While I was gone, did Charles Skinner come back and get his fountain pen?'

She nodded again. She looked like she was anxious to be helpful.

'So Charles Skinner came back and took that fountain pen?' I said, amazed she should admit it.

'Yes,' she said. 'Is there anything wrong in that?'

I got up and roared at her. 'Then why the hell did you say this morning he went away without it?'

'But he did,' she said. 'He went away without it. Came back a few minutes later for it.'

'Why in hell didn't you say so?' I roared.

She looked at me surprised, just a little indignant. 'That's what I wanted to tell you this morning,' she argued. 'But you put the words into my mouth. You wanted me to say he went away without it and that was all. You wouldn't let me say he came back.'

I raised my eyes to heaven, clenched my fists and beat them against my chest. 'Of all the dumb dames,' I said bitterly.

'Don't you call me dumb!' she said shrilly.

'Why couldn't you tell me this morning?' I said. 'All this trouble, all this worry, all on account of you not speaking the truth.'

'I did what you asked me,' she protested. 'Don't you remember how careful you were to make me repeat it? I had to say it word for word.'

'Jeepers!' I muttered to myself. I paced up and down the room. Then saw the bedroom door, which was partly open, move a fraction. I remembered about the hat. I remembered, too, that Lulu knew a whole lot more about the *Chronicle* business than it was safe for the police to know.

I walked over to the bedroom door, wrenched it open. The guy who was in there musta scampered across the room, climbed under the sheets and covered himself.

My eyes roved around the room. Lulu came in after me, protesting. 'It's not what you think, Hank, really. I mean – I mean –' She faltered. Then, defensively: 'Well, I've got to have some friends, haven't I? And I did ask you.'

'Shuddup,' I said.

'I was going to get rid of him because of you –'

'Shuddup!' I said again.

There were a jacket, trousers and underclothes hanging over a chair. I recognised those, too. I picked them up, stuffed them under my arm.

'All right, Sharp,' I said. 'You can come out. I know you're there.'

His red face came up over the sheet. He glared at me viciously.

'You pimp!' I said bitingly. 'That's the kinda fella you are! Going around preaching morality! And this is the kinda thing you do!'

'You ain't gonna get away with this, Janson!' he threatened. 'I heard what you were saying to this dame. Trying to fix evidence. Concealing evidence. It's gonna mean real trouble for you!'

I retreated towards the door, still keeping his clothes under my arm.

'You know the law as well as I do, Sharp,' I said. 'Anything you say doesn't mean a thing. You've gotta have witnesses, and as for what went on in our office this morning, my Chief and I don't know a thing about it. As far as we're concerned, this dame never existed.'

'I'll get you some way, Janson!' he threatened. 'I'll be lucky if I can hold down my job after this. I'll get you for it!'

'You tried to do that once before,' I sneered. 'You got what was coming to you.'

I was still backing towards the door. Suddenly he realised what I was doing.

'Hey!' he yelled. 'My clothes!'

'You're gonna lose those, brother,' I said.

He made a sudden spring for me. I'd never seen him without clothes before. I managed to shut the bedroom door and lock it before I began to laugh uncontrollably. You'd have laughed too! Without clothes he looked like a guy who'd been in Belsen for a century or so.

'You mustn't do that,' said Lulu. 'You must let him have his clothes back.'

'Listen, honey,' I said. 'I'm gonna do you a favour. That guy can't get out of here without clothes. And just as long as he's without clothes you're gonna be happy. I'm gonna make you happy, honey. See?'

'But I don't want him, Hank,' she said earnestly. 'I want you.'

'But I'm busy, honey,' I said. 'Can't you make do with him until I come back?'

'Will you be long?' she pouted.

'Not too long,' I said.

She was still pleading with me all the way to the door to come back soon. She didn't plead too hard, though. I guessed that having one guy staked out ready was occupying her mind.

There was a post office nearby. I borrowed paper and string and made up a parcel of the clothes. I addressed it to Conrad, c/o Police Headquarters, and sent it parcel post. I guessed Sharp would have difficulty explaining that away.

Then I went home.

14

I was fitting the key into the lock of my apartment when a soft voice at my elbow said: 'Hello, Hank.'

I looked up wearily. 'Hello, Stella,' I said.

She didn't wait to be asked in. She pushed inside with me. The pain in my head was starting again. I shuffled through into the living-room, switched on the light, sank down in a chair and eased the shoes off my feet.

'May I come in?' asked Stella. She was already in.

'Get me a drink, will you?' I said. I nodded towards the cocktail cabinet.

'Straight or soda?'

'Straight.'

She poured a coupla drinks, came over, sat down beside me. She eased her bolero off her shoulders and she was wearing a plain red frock with a neckline that plunged to her waist.

'I wanna talk to you, Hank,' she said.

'Do you have to?'

'If you don't mind.' She smiled sweetly and looked at me with her face tilted on one side. It made her red hair ripple over her shoulders. I bet she knew that.

'Look, Stella,' I said. 'I'm worn out. I had one hour's sleep last night. Since then I've been chasing murderers all over town. I've had umpteen false leads. I've been pushed around by cops, smacked in the teeth, worried till my brain is withered to a dried pod and every bone in my body is aching. I've got the grandfather of all headaches, a blood-pressure that's way up level with Everest, and a hunger that's gnawing the pit of my stomach. I've just remembered I haven't eaten all day.'

'I'm sorry, Hank,' she said sympathetically. She got a bright idea.

'Look, honey. Why don't you stretch out on the settee. Make yourself comfortable. If you've got anything in the icebox, I'll scramble a meal.'

That sounded a whole lot better than talking. 'That's fine!' I said. I took her advice, spread out the cushions on the settee, took off my jacket, stretched myself out and sighed with relief.

Stella disappeared into the kitchen. I lay there, drowsily fighting off sleep. Not long after, she returned with a tray of food. Fried bacon, fried eggs, marmalade, toast and coffee.

I took time off to eat the food, and it sure tasted good. Finally, with a sigh of satisfaction, I lapsed back on the cushions. She cleared away the dishes, manoeuvred a hassock into position by the side of the settee and sat down. The way she was sitting facing me, I could see between the cleavage of her breasts nearly down to her navel.

'I want to ask your advice, Hank,' she said solemnly.

'If it's worth anything.'

'I'm sure it is, honey,' she said. 'I think you'll give

good advice.'

'If I stay awake long enough to give it.'

'It's about Dane,' she said.

I closed my eyes. 'What about him?' I mumbled.

'I was a fool,' she said bitterly. 'What a fool I made of myself with Burden. And now I see it quite clearly. Dane was so good. He was so thoughtful. He thought the world of me. And he did everything he could to stop me being so foolish.' There was a sob in her voice. 'I guess I just didn't understand.'

'I could have told you that last night,' I said. 'But you weren't in the mood to take advice then.'

'I know,' she said humbly. 'I must have been out of my mind.'

I opened my eyes, looked at her. She was thinking over what had happened the previous night. I could tell right away if ever a dame was sorry for something, it was Stella.

'Well, what about Dane?'

'I want you to help me, Hank,' she said softly.

'How? What can I do?'

'Make him understand,' she said. 'He'll listen to you. Explain I wasn't myself. Tell him I didn't know what I was doing.'

'What good will that do?'

'I'm so lonely now, Hank,' she said. 'I don't know what I'll do without him. I didn't realise how much I'd begun to rely on him.'

I eased myself up on one elbow and stared at her. 'You don't know yet, then?'

'Don't know what?'

I breathed heavily. 'Dane's in Las Vegas,' I said.

'Las Vegas?' Her eyebrows arched. 'Is there some festival on there?'

'Why do people usually go to Las Vegas?' I asked.

'They usually go there to get married quickly,' she said. 'But Dane wouldn't be doing that ...' She broke off, and her wide eyes stared at me with sudden alarm.

'You've hit it,' I said. 'That's why he's gone.'

'No,' she breathed, incredulously.

'You lost out on that one,' I said.

'But he couldn't. He couldn't have done that!' she pleaded.

'He's done it,' I said brutally. 'And I guess it won't work out too badly at that.'

'But who was it?' she asked. 'There was nobody he knew. I was the only one.' .

'Up until last night,' I said. 'What you did last night kinda opened his eyes. He looked around. He found something else that suited him better.'

'Better!'

'Sure,' I said. 'You don't think anybody could treat him worse than you did?'

'But who was she?'

'Just a dame,' I said. 'Just a dame named Pearl Gibbons. You wouldn't know her.'

'She was at the party ...'

'That's where he met her.'

Her cheeks flamed. Her eyes flashed angrily. 'Cheap chiseller,' she said bitterly. 'Just to meet a girl like that at a party! Leaves me high and dry and marries her! Just like that! Hardly known her a minute!'

I chuckled.

She glared at me. 'What's so funny?'

'Figure it out, honey. You gave him the air. You treated him as badly as a dame can treat a guy. He goes somewhere else for sympathy and gets it. He laps up the sympathy like a cat laps up milk. He can't get enough of it. So he dashes off to Las Vegas to stake out a claim for a perpetual supply. Can you blame him?'

She dropped her eyes, suddenly humble. 'Guess not,' she admitted.

'Get me another drink, will ya, honey?' I said.

'Of course,' she said softly.

She got up quickly, handling herself carelessly. She had been sitting on a low hassock. The way her skirts whirled around showed a lot of her thigh. I watched her as she walked across the room. She had a nice way of walking, a kinda animated walk with a gentle, fascinating swing of the haunches. I watched as she poured the drink. Her red hair hung across her forehead and cheek like a red cloud, and her firm breasts pressed outward against her dress. When she straightened up she saw me watching her, and there musta been something special about the way I was watching her. She blushed slightly and a pleased smile came to her lips.

She brought the drinks back, sat down again, and somehow there was a difference in the atmosphere. Almost as though there was an understanding between us.

'You give me ideas,' I said. 'I'm gonna get rid of all my chairs and have only hassocks for my girlfriends to sit on.'

'Why's that?' she chuckled. Her eyes smiled into mine.

'Well,' I said, and looked meaningfully at her legs. 'It kinda improves the view.'

'Anything you haven't seen, Hank?' she asked pointedly.

'I've got to admit it, Stella,' I said. 'You've got nice legs.'

'You really think so, Hank?' She pushed her legs

straight out in front of her, pulled her skirts so they rode over her knees and examined her legs critically.

'Yeah,' I said. 'Real nice.'

'I'm glad you think so, Hank,' she said. She left her skirt where it was and doubled up her legs again. That meant the hem of her skirt fell back into her lap. She looked at me with soft, dreamy eyes. 'You're so understanding, Hank,' she said.

'I wish I were,' I said. 'I really wish I were.'

'But you are!'

'There's lots of things I don't understand,' I said. 'Why dames do things. Why guys do things. Why I let you sit here talking to me this way, why I'm admiring your legs and finding I'm really liking you, while all the time I know you're a first-class bitch.'

She didn't get annoyed. 'You don't really think so, do you, Hank?' she asked pleadingly.

'A quarter of an hour ago, I did,' I said. 'I'm not so sure now,' and I looked at her warm, sleek thighs. 'My judgment's biased right now.'

She chuckled deep down in her throat. 'You and me are the same kinda people, aren't we, Hank?'

'Are we?'

'You take life as it comes. You don't quarrel with life. We just accept it.'

'I duck and dodge occasionally,' I said. I looked at her legs again. 'Whenever I've got the moral courage.'

The hem of her skirt was in her lap. She held it there with one hand while she changed position, transferred from the hassock to the edge of the settee. When she was sitting beside me that way I could see along her thighs into the shadows of her soft, filmy underwear.

'I'm tired, Stella,' I said. 'I had one hour's sleep last

night. I've been slogging all day. I'm worn out.'

'Poor boy,' she said. She leaned over and stroked my forehead gently, smoothed my hair back. It was nice.

I nodded. 'It's nice,' I said. 'It's soothing.'

She was leaning over me. Her plunging neckline revealed milky white skin. Her breasts were pointed strong and firm. 'You don't believe in uplift?' I said softly.

'Of course not, honey. You don't think I need it, do you?'

'Lots of dames do,' I said. 'It's supposed to do something for their figure.'

She was still stroking my forehead, softly, gently, smoothing back my hair. My tired limbs weren't aching anymore, they seemed to have eased into restful relaxation.

'I never have needed uplift,' she said. 'Did you think I did?' Her eyes were smiling into mine.

'I just wondered,' I said.

'I can prove it,' she said.

'I guess so,' I said. 'I …'

She was fumbling with the lower button at the front of her dress. The neckline widened a lot more and showed clearly the firm, hard thrust of her breasts against the dress. Without a doubt they were firm enough to require no dressmaker's aids.

'You sure are cute,' I said softly, tiredly.

Her hand was like cool velvet caressing my forehead, caressing my hair.

With her other hand she eased the dress off her shoulders, allowing it to slip down her upper arms so that her warm, tautened breasts were pointing towards me. Her eyes were suddenly hot and sulky. She said harshly like she couldn't breathe properly: 'There's something about you, Hank.'

'That's nice, honey,' I said. 'So soothing. Don't stop.'

Her cool hand still gently stroked my forehead. And her other hand was suddenly urgently busy, unbuttoning the frock front, loosening it from around her.

Just for a moment she stopped stroking my forehead while she entirely discarded the frock. Then she was crouched alongside me, her face looking down into mine, the soft white flesh of her waist enveloped in a mysterious haze of frothy underclothing, smooth sleek thighs quivering with an urgent strength and glistening beneath the lights.

'It's nice,' I said dreamily. 'Don't stop.'

Her cool fingers caressed my forehead again. It soothed my aching head.

It was cleansing like cool water washing away sweaty perspiration. My body was tired, my limbs were tired, my brain was tired. And suddenly it was like lying on a cloud. There was a gentle breeze blowing on me and the soft sun warming me. There was soft music dreaming in my ears and a pleasant stimulation of my emotions.

Hot smoky eyes were staring down into mine. Her teeth were white between moist, parted lips. My eyes brushed between the hard, vibrant curve of her breasts, over the soft skin of her belly to where her hand was fumbling with that mysterious concealing froth of underclothing that was miraculously and slowly slipping away to reveal more mysterious and subtle curves.

Her cool hand was still gently caressing my forehead. I was still on a cloud. There was still soft music in my ears and a soft, gentle stimulation of my emotions.

Her hot eyes stared down into mine. 'Hank,' she said hoarsely. 'Won't you ... can't you ...?' her voice broke off into a kinda moan, and as she wriggled her body, silk rippled along her thighs, over her knees and around her ankles.

'Hank,' she said fiercely, and she gave a kinda fierce moan. 'I want you, Hank.'

My eyes slipped between the cleavage of her breasts towards dark, subtle hollows. Her cool hand still gently caressed my forehead. The cloud was a beautiful whirl of soft emotion, soft music and peace.

I fell asleep.

ALSO AVAILABLE FROM TELOS PUBLISHING

CRIME

THE LONG, BIG KISS GOODBYE
by SCOTT MONTGOMERY
Hardboiled thrills as Jack Sharp gets involved with a
dame called Kitty.

MIKE RIPLEY

Titles in Mike Ripley's acclaimed 'Angel' series of comic
crime novels.

JUST ANOTHER ANGEL by MIKE RIPLEY
ANGEL TOUCH by MIKE RIPLEY
ANGEL HUNT by MIKE RIPLEY
ANGEL ON THE INSIDE by MIKE RIPLEY
ANGEL CONFIDENTIAL by MIKE RIPLEY
ANGEL CITY by MIKE RIPLEY
ANGELS IN ARMS by MIKE RIPLEY
FAMILY OF ANGELS by MIKE RIPLEY
BOOTLEGGED ANGEL by MIKE RIPLEY
THAT ANGEL LOOK by MIKE RIPLEY

HANK JANSON

Classic pulp crime thrillers from the 1940s and 1950s.

TORMENT by HANK JANSON
WOMEN HATE TILL DEATH by HANK JANSON

SOME LOOK BETTER DEAD by HANK JANSON
SKIRTS BRING ME SORROW by HANK JANSON
WHEN DAMES GET TOUGH by HANK JANSON
ACCUSED by HANK JANSON
KILLER by HANK JANSON
FRAILS CAN BE SO TOUGH by HANK JANSON
BROADS DON'T SCARE EASY by HANK JANSON
KILL HER IF YOU CAN by HANK JANSON
LILIES FOR MY LOVELY by HANK JANSON
BLONDE ON THE SPOT by HANK JANSON
THIS WOMAN IS DEATH by HANK JANSON
THE LADY HAS A SCAR by HANK JANSON

Non-fiction

THE TRIALS OF HANK JANSON
by STEVE HOLLAND

TELOS PUBLISHING
Email: orders@telos.co.uk
Web: www.telos.co.uk

To order copies of any Telos books, please visit our
website where there are full details of all titles and
facilities for worldwide credit card online ordering, as
well as occasional special offers.

CPSIA information can be obtained
at www.ICGtesting.com
Printed in the USA
LVOW01s2344101115
461894LV00031B/1098/P